Women R Stupid

&

Men R The

Reason

Steven Barthell

Aziza Publishing
Boston, Massachusetts

Aziza Publishing LLC
170 Ashmont Street, Boston, MA 02124

Women R Stupid & Men R The Reason

An Aziza Publishing Book/ published by arrangement with the author

PRINTING HISTORY
Aziza Publishing mass-market edition/ February 2011

Copyright © 2011 Steven Barthell
Edited by Aquila Butler
Cover Design by STAE TRU
Photography by Bryan Trench
Text design by Rochelle Levy
Author Photo by Tiarah Thomas of Miss B Photography

For more information write to: Aziza Publishing LLC
170 Ashmont Street, Suite 16, Boston, MA 02124

ISBN: 978-0-615-45277-7

PRINTED IN THE UNITED STATES OF AMERICA

2011903036

"Success is liking yourself, liking what you do, and liking how you do it."
~Maya Angelou

I dedicate this book to my late aunt Ruthy Woolley and other family members and friends I have lost who couldn't wait to see my dream come true.

My sister Jannell Taylor and my mother Harriet L. Taylor; the two most important women in my life.

CONTENTS

Acknowledgments

ACKNOWLEDGMENTS

First and foremost, I have to give honor to God: He has been the best tag team partner in my life, and has never given up on me. I never would have made it without His faith in me and without Him making sure I did not lose sight of the important things in life. He and I have been through storms together. Storms He strategically placed in my life to see if I was able to get through them, and I am not finished yet. I thank you Lord for life, for the truth about myself, and helping megrow to be the man You want me to be. There is nobody like You Lord, and I thank you so much for everything. You are God alone and no one will ever be more important in my life because I have learned through You anything is possible.

I thank both of my parents Harriet Taylor and Howard White for creating me, along with Reginald Taylor for helping to raise me. Even though I have my own personal thoughts about my father, I have learned how to forgive and forget, and will have no hate in my body. I love you and I pray for you. My mother has been my biggest supporter and my biggest fan since I was placed into her arms at Boston Medical on that cool night of May 16th, 1984. I love you Ma, and we did it baby! It's time for the dreams to come true and the blessings to start pouring. Reggie, you and I talk sporadically to this day, and I thank you for all the knowledge you put into my brain; it is very much appreciated, and I respect you for the willingness to take care of another man's child.

My brother and sister, Reggie and Jannell Taylor, I love you both dearly. Jannell you grow very fast with your experiences and will make an excellent wife one day; you always have my back and have the passion I want to match each activity I pursue. Reggie you are on your way to becoming a huge media source; not only in Boston, Massachusetts, but soon nation and worldwide. I have no doubts that my brother will stand side by side with me as we take our generation by the neck and shake up the world.

To the Barthell, White and Taylor Family. There are so many of you and I LOVE each and every one of you, no more or less than the next one. I know I can be a pain in the ass and have jokes for days, but you have always believed in me; with each cookout that I show out at and each event I wanted you guys to attend. I thank you for them all. I will never forget where I came from and will not lose the knowledge you placed upon me. I love you all.

To the Best Crew in the World: Melvin Casseus, Leighton Lormeus, Julie Rivera and Guy Andre; Juan Harnett, Luckner Alteon and Jeff Jean Baptiste, you have been my brothers and sister in the world. Even though some of us have fell off with one another, you guys have been the reason why I push and work hard every day, and why I write the things that I do. From drama to celebration; from sadness to smiles, thank you for being family without the blood.

To my publisher Aziza Publishing, and its president Rochelle Levy; thank you for believing in my talents. I was a man with a voice and no leader to guide me. You have shown me the tough consistent love that I needed to accomplish my first journey. Even though these were my words in the book, it was your kick in the ass that really made it happen. I love you so much for that.

Social Networks Facebook, Twitter, YouTube and MySpace; I owe my popularity to having the opportunity to place videos, and say what I want, on the internet.

To Jackie Martinez (Lust & Sassy Entertainment), thank you for being my manager for five minutes. In all seriousness, thank you for battling with me and making sure I stayed on my toes. I love you like my sister, and your many siblings are lucky to have you as a member of their family. **Get it Daddy**

To Bryan "Avi Mr. Superfly" Trench; brother you have been promoting me since we first met in the now defunct club 360 in Boston, Massachusetts. Thank you for having a huge heart sir, even though the world says we both aren't shit (inside joke). I give credit where it is due with the creative process of promoting this book, and not caring what the social networks have to say about me. You are an excellent motivator, producer, young entrepreneur and even better friend. Stae Tru is the truth!

Tiarah Thomas and Miss B Photography, you are naturally talented and a great supporter. I am proud of you with everything you're doing behind the camera.

I thank the artist and other Stae Tru rep, Mr. Dee Loopz; thank you for the inspiration and cover work; brother you are truly a blessed and talented, great writer and performer. Stay blessed and Stae Tru my friend.

My mentor and father figure David Wright; oh, man I can fill this whole page but I know you wouldn't want that, so I'll simply say thank you Pop! It's time for the David Wright initiative to take off.

Sheila "Nefertiti" Montas, thank you for the support, and for gracing the cover with your beauty and intelligence. You are on your way to doing big things within the community of Boston and throughout the media. I am proud of the hard work you are putting in.

To the Shine Staff: Tiffany Starr Traynham, Lillie D, and Regina Seale. Thank you for helping me to show off my talents and taking me seriously; even though I'm always clowning on set and during meetings. I love you ladies, and Shine is going to be a great success.

Wow, there are so many other names and groups to thank and shout out. I know I said I was going to do individual shout outs, but I can't because it will not be fair to people who I forget or don't mention. Thank you everybody who has supported me throughout the five to six year journey of writing this book. To all the promotional groups flooding my Facebook or Twitter; THANK YOU for the love in the clubs and the lounges.

Thank you to all of the supporters on my fan and support page; you all keep me pushing and make me want to do better.

Thank you for all my friends throughout my childhood, school and my adult life.

Thank you to all the people who didn't think I was going to be able to complete this project and to those who have no belief in my abilities. THANK YOU EVERYBODY!

PROLOGUE

Dear Ladies and Gentlemen:

I love you with all of my heart, but some of you are fucking stupid! You are fucking up! If you think I am talking about you, then I probably am. Block out the profane language; open up your hearts and minds, and hear me out before you get defensive.

In this book, I will give you the tools to escape the trials and tribulations life gives you. We are going to discuss how to prevent and stabilize certain situations. We will travel through Little Nigga University and show you how to shut that son of a bitch down! You will learn the art of courtship, the art of grinding it out and you will learn how to get rid of the ridiculous annoying ass tendencies in your life-or simply get rid of the RAATs. Are you ready for the beginning of the next step of getting your shit together? Then, in the words of my grandfather, "LETGO!"

~Steven

LADIES

This section is dedicated to the women who are satisfied with being someone's "baby mama," accepting a man calling you a bitch, playing your position, and being a man's booty call. This is for the women who would rather find their way to "free before 11 o'clock" at the club, instead of spending quality time with their spouse, child or children; who would rather collect from the state for years instead of pushing forward to earn an income. This message is for every woman who says, "men ain't shit." Well you're right about that because—MEN ARE HUMANS! The beginning of this book is to call you stupid, not because you are, but just to rattle you until it gets through to your brain that life isn't a fucking game!

When will you realize that you are a queen? You were placed on this earth to not only help reproduce, but to help lead our society to heights we can only imagine. I understand that a man probably did to you what we only see in movies. He probably made you feel low, hit you, ran off and left you alone with the kids; made you feel like you were only good for sex and nothing more. I know from experience that you probably grew up with no strong female or male figure to teach you how to be a lady at all times.

You probably have a shield over your heart, don't you? Yeah, I can see right through it. Believe me when I say it is healable and can be restored. I know you have probably seen it all and heard it all. You have probably heard every single line in the book. From, "Baby, let me hold you, touch you, and I love you," to "you ain't shit, you're ugly, you're only good enough to make babies or for laying on your back." I want to apologize on the behalf of all men. I only do this because women are the most precious things on this earth. There is nothing like a woman! Even though I don't understand you sometimes, and y'all drive me to say things like, "Women are fucking stupid," you do have to understand that most men don't know how to treat you; but it's not their fault. I can't justify anyone's actions, but some men will never learn how to treat you; so be careful who you give your time,

4

heart and energy to. Most men didn't have the upbringing to talk to you the right way or to treat you the right way, but if he does, **DON'T BE AFRAID TO BE HAPPY!** I know times are rough and you feel as if you need to have a huge brick wall over your pretty little heart, but trust me, **ALL MEN AREN'T THE SAME**. I know you have heard it all, and you have seen it all, but true love does exist. It's a beautiful thing when it happens, but people overall have lost the true meaning of what love is supposed to be about. Love is about finding a new experience with someone you never thought you would meet; someone who turns your life around completely. It's not a weekend thing or just a temporary thing. I tell people all the time, "Please don't use it just to use it; you'll ruin someone's life." As a matter of fact, you'll ruin three lives-yours, the person who you said it to and didn't mean it, and the next person who will truly mean it—so be careful with the words I love you.

Why is it that every time a relationship doesn't go your way, you build a huge wall over yourself? Okay, let's pause for a second. I will leave the relationship issues for the later chapters, but I will say this. Ladies, if you want to prevent getting your heart broken so easily, then stop giving it away so easily. I know it's easier said than done, but taking your time, asking questions and demanding respect is a great way to prevent yourself from going through the "all men ain't shit, I'm never falling in love, I'll go get a girlfriend instead; I can raise children by myself. Fuck him, him and him!" blues. Once again ladies; you all are queens! Queens who are here to make sure the kings of this earth get the job right.

Ladies, you are better than how society portrays you. You are more than eye candy, you shouldn't have to raise kids by yourself, and you are far greater than shaking your ass for a piece of change just to entertain men. You don't have to keep participating in "Drop it Low" contests, because being a model doesn't mean showing your ass first and your face last. You are the greatest creation God has come up with—a WOMAN—so stop trying to be someone that you're not— a MAN. I hear the saying, "think like a man before you get played like a bitch," all the time, but guess what? You are not a bitch! So, why are you worried about getting played like one? You are gorgeous, so stop acting ugly.

At this point, I can hear the "he's not talking about me" chants. While I may not be talking to you as an individual, I am talking to you as an entire sex. I see women put each other down, instead of stepping in and helping their sisters out. I use the word sister because in God's eyes, we are all family; get the race card out of your head. If you are sitting next to someone right now—go ahead look, I'll wait—look at them closely. Have you walked in their shoes? No? Okay, stop judging, because you have no idea what that person is going through; maybe if you take the time out to see if you can help, you will be putting your energy to better use than judging them. Ladies, when a man calls you a "bitch" how do you feel? Do you get mad, or do you brush it off? Do you respond or acknowledge that he is speaking to you? It doesn't matter that, since you ladies call each other "bitch," you might think it's common, thus making it okay. The word "bitch" was created to degrade you; it was made up to put you down and some ass clown started using it to describe you, in order to make himself or herself feel better. The same applies to the words hoe, slut, bish, whore, etcetera. You are you; so demand to be called by your birth name, or even a nickname, but don't settle to be called something you are not. Even though I called you fucking stupid, you must admit it gave you a great reason to keep reading right? YES! Moving on...

Ladies, you know what else? Men aren't the only ones not taking care of their children; some of you would rather hit up a local club, bar or lounge than spend quality time with the little one(s). Yes, you need your "me" time, but "me" time should be a little more creative than partying every Friday, Saturday, or Sunday. As quiet as it's kept, some will find every and any excuse to party Tuesday thru Sunday. "I'm going to party to make up for what I lost." What in the blue hell does that mean? You were pregnant for only nine months or less; add on a few more months that you may have used to lose pregnancy weight, and then you're back in the party scene? What part of the game is this? Set an example for your damn kids; maybe if he or she were familiar with words other than, "the babysitter is here" or "Mama will be back" coming from your mouth, he or she wouldn't be a troubled child. Some of you don't even cook anymore. When was the last time your child had a decent home-cooked meal that you prepared? Warming up Beefaroni or making noodles isn't gonna cut it five nights a week. During a child's first few years in this world, he or she needs their mother at all times. Yes, I will be much harder on the fellas, but this isn't their turn to get yelled at.

So what have you learned so far? Take pride in being a woman, demand respect from men and other women, take care of your kids and realize you are the greatest creation God has made. EVER! Ladies, if you want to be the "Queen of the Spades" I'm going to need you to stop acting like the eight of clubs.

FELLAS

F ELLAS, what the fuck is wrong with you? Why are we catching all of the blame for society's problems? Why must we act like we don't give two shits and an apple pie about life? Why do some of us pretend that we are in a rap video or living the life of our favorite "hood" movie? This is real life, and we have to take responsibility for our actions at all times! I'm tired of you degrading women. I'm sick of hearing, "I'm grinding", "M.O.B-- Money over Bitches", "Trust no bitch", " _INSERT RAPPER'S NAME HERE _says I should_ INSERT HIP-HOP QUOTE HERE_," etcetera. Why is money and getting sex our top priority? Is it because someone on television, whom we haven't met, or may never meet, said to do so? Just as I told the ladies, you too are royalty. You are a king! So stop acting like a joker. We are here to pave the path, and build on this world we call earth. Chasing money does nothing but blind you from the bigger picture of life, which includes success, family, wealth—please note that there's a major difference between being rich and wealthy—and getting to heaven. Worshiping those dead white guys on green paper will leave you with a dark life.

When did it become cool to "hold the block down" every single night? Why aren't we taking care of our child or children? Take responsibility for your actions especially when it comes to children. They did not ask you to not use protection and get their mother knocked up. That was your choice; why? Because it felt good? Because you think you are a grown ass man? If that's the case, act like it. Stop giving these women an excuse to call you what you are not, but are pretending to be—weak. You are strong; you are intelligent, you are a man! Why would you want another to swoop in and do something you are not doing? When you shy away from you responsibilities, that does make you appear weak, punkish and as if you are a failure. You don't have to become that. You have the choice and the chance to be something far more greater than a "baby's Daddy." You can become a father. That title is exceedingly stronger than sperm donor, that motherfucker, "HIM," etc.

Dude, you are intelligent! You are not what society says you are; you're not a thug, you're not a goon, you're not a punk, and you're not a popular actor in the movies, (unless of course you actually are the latter). In our society, terminology is a major factor. Do you think a corporation or any employer wants to hire a "goon?" I know you are out there grinding, but how are you grinding, and what are you grinding for? Did you know that the art of grinding is supposed to advance you in life? Not put you in situations where you will be in jail for 20 to life! Fellas, it's time to kick it up a notch and dare to be different.

I know that some women put you down and make you feel as if you are not the man you really are, but I'm going to tell you something that helped me. Be who you want to be, and not what other people want you to be. Take that however you want to, but you cannot continue to give yourself a bad name. When you hit those streets, you represent yourself, your family and its legacy. If the legacy isn't that much to talk about, change the game and make it worth it. No more excuses. Fuck that. You were not placed on this earth for that. You are here because God wants you rule it and take charge. You are here to have the courage to make a difference, and you are here to take the knowledge you received and pass it along to other boys so they can become men. Therefore, **GET YOUR SHIT TOGETHER!**

Furthermore, financially, easy money isn't smart money; even if you think you have it down pat. Thinking this way hinders you from realizing the things you have the potential to attain. God sees you hustling for that easy money; He may allow you to think you're balling, but name one successful drug dealer, thief, mob boss, or murderer that has gotten off? Maybe they did on Earth, but once they approach those pearly gates, it's doomsday. Can you imagine walking up to the gates of heaven and being turned away? That would be beyond embarrassing! Visualize the conversation: "John Doe, for 10 years, you were a successful drug dealer polluting your city or state with tons of temporary fixes, but I am the permanent fix. I was the solution and you helped the enemy, the devil, blind my children. I forgive you, but you ruined lives; your drugs killed people. You took matters of finances into your own hands; therefore, I have to turn you away." Do you want that? I have never ever heard of a human bringing money, cars or sexual partners with them into heaven. Stop thinking small; DREAM BIG, or don't dream at all. You are so talented that you can be whoever you want to be, and you have the ability to grow, even as a grown ass man.

On another note, stop lying to these women; be upfront and keep it real. Do you really want to be the reason why one woman hates all men? All men?!? Do you want that burden on your heart? Know what you want fellas; be able to meet her half way and beyond with those same expectations you require of her. What I want you to do right now is make a list of the qualities you are looking for in a woman. No, it's not lame. It's actually helpful, so trust me. I'm a witness, and here's an example below:

SHE HAS TO BE TRUE TO HERSELF

If a woman doesn't first believe in herself, what makes you think she is going to believe in you?

SHE HAS TO BE HONEST

People make mistakes and tell little white lies, but if a person can't look you in your eyes and tell the truth at least 99.9% of the time, then it is not worth messing with them.

SHE HAS TO SHOW AFFECTION

Not saying to be all over your loved one 24/7, but she should at least show that she cares for you. Not only physically, but also mentally and spiritually; if she can't do that, what's the point of a commitment? You may as well have a friendship, which gets to my next point.

SHE HAS TO BE WILLING TO BE YOUR BEST FRIEND ESPECIALLY WITH COMMUNICATION

Being able to talk to your loved one should be relaxing and fun. There shouldn't be any secrets between the two of you. Now I know there are things you and friends talk about that are supposed to stay between the crew; that's cool, but for the most part, your partner should be filled in on the things that mostly pertain to you.

SHE HAS TO KNOW WHAT SHE WANTS OUT OF YOUR RELATIONSHIP

Don't pressure the woman, but don't waste your or her time either. If you both aren't on the same page about how to deal with your relationship, then you're fresh out of luck. You'll end up sitting there watching your damn phone, wondering if she's gonna call. Or you'll be thinking "hey she's about to be "wifey"" while she's thinking she's found another BFF!

SHE HAS TO BE INDEPENDENT

An independent woman gives off a major attraction, but sometimes that independence has its disadvantages. You want someone who is going to take care of herself, but you also want someone who is going to let you take care of her when she can't, and also have the willingness to accept happiness. If a woman is letting her past reflect her future, RUN NIGGA RUN!

SHE HAS TO ACCEPT YOU FOR YOU

She got into the relationship for a reason and if she can't accept you for who you are, then there's a problem; especially if there was no negative change in your attitude. There is always room for change, if it's for the betterment of the entire relationship. However, you're an adult, and your personality is established already! I'm tired of people thinking they can change others. You cannot change them, so what the fuck?!

SHE HAS TO HAVE A BALANCED LIFE

I have seen some women who would do anything in their power to get a baby sitter for the dumbest shit ever, or to party all the damn time. Nobody wants a party girl. Nobody wants a temporary mom, and nobody wants a temporary girlfriend. There is nothing wrong with going out and having a good time, but if every weekend you'd rather party and not spend quality time with me, SEEFUCKYALATA!

SHE HAS TO KNOW HOW TO COOK

A way to a man's heart is through his stomach (VERY TRUE)!

There are plenty more things I could list, but those are my basics; as a man you have to define yours. I'm not that hard to please, but it's hard finding a woman who fits the bill for 85% of this list. With me, it's almost like qualifying for a job; there is the application, interview, and the probationary period. Shit, I know women treat men the same way, but in a worse way. I have heard, "he's cool now, but eventually he'll show his true colors." I'm far from perfect, but what you see is what you get. I'm not changing for you, you, you, or you! I'M ME! Don't like it? Well, you know the rest.

So, that's my list and I'm sticking to it fellas. As a reminder, I will ask again. What are you willing to give back? If you are not sure, create a list. Below is an example:

WHEN I GET A GIRLFRIEND/FUTURE WIFE, SHE WILL GET THE FOLLOWING:

1. **A MAN** that doesn't need to be reminded that you are here for me, and you are not going anywhere; you know what I'm talking about—all the silly questions to remind him that his penis is working. Like, "Baby do you love me? You didn't say it back," or "What are you doing? Who's over there with y'all?" How about this one, "Who was better, me or him?" It sounds silly, but you'd be surprised by the insecurity of some of the people who I hang around, and use to hang around. I was once that man!

2. **A MAN** who calls to see how your day is going, and not calling to check up on you, I will be sincere about the call and every now and again, I might just surprise you with lunch or dinner at work or home when you least expect it; without violating your "me" time, of course.

3. **A MAN** that can look you in the eyes without hesitation and tell you his whereabouts, and not be lying for a change. Trust me, we are all not the same. Of course we all make mistakes and slip here and

there, but when you have someone who is honest with you at all times that's special!!

4. **A MAN** who is willing to accept his mistakes and try his best to learn from them... He can even admit that, "Hey I fucked up!!!! I'm sorry, and I will make sure the shit doesn't happen again."

5. **A MAN** who is willing to make sure you are okay in the bedroom before himself. In my opinion, being selfish went out the door in 1998 with the Chicago Bull Dynasty.

6. **A MAN** who can say, "Babe, I'm going out with the guys to..." either play ball, go to the club, play video games, or just chill, and he WON'T LIE ABOUT IT!!!!!

7. **A MAN** that can cook his ass off. Oh my gosh, do I need to go any further on this one?

8. **A MAN** who knows that he should go to church, and *stop cursing*, but is *still working on it*!!

What I wrote might not be exactly how you feel, and vice versa, but having a plan with these women helps. It also gives you an idea of how you want to proceed with your relationship so, *no excuses*!

LADIES AND GENTLEMEN

L ife has its struggles and has its ups and downs. To tell the truth, shit happens; but overall, it's all about how you wipe your ass. You do not have to live the life of a fake baller, playboy, millionaire, billionaire, video vixen, pin up model or whatever they're calling themselves. After reading this, did it make you open your eyes? Are you mad at me because I had the guts to call you stupid. Did it make you realize that now it's time to wake the fuck up? I know you're human and we all make mistakes. If you   are doing what you are supposed to do in life, and are thinking, "Okay, I'm good Steven," kick it up a notch! Why settle for being just good, when you can be *great*?! If no one has ever told you that they care for you, I'm here pouring my heart out to you. Ladies and gentlemen, it's time for a change! No, I am not talking to every man or woman in the world about the few things I have stated in this opening chapter, but the majority of you are fucking up; yeah, I said it. You are fucking up! Now get it together before it's too late.

WELCOME TO L.N.U.
(LITTLE NI**A UNIVERSITY)

I want you to, once again, open up your hearts and minds. Throw your race, the color of your skin, where you grew up, your age, your sex and thought process out of the window. We live in a world where we blame each other for why we don't have total peace and tranquility. However, I'm going to take you into a world where it's okay to disrespect your peers and elders. Let's go to a place where skinny jeans have replaced baggy ones, although the jeans don't seem like a major difference to me besides the size; where women wear leggings into the work place. Where a parent feels as if striking the fear of God into their children is wrong. Where it's cool to pay twenty dollars to party or just post up on the club's wall. You are about to enter a world where speaking your mind about your wants and needs is looked down upon; where having money is the motive behind people's actions, rather than happiness, families, getting to heaven and giving back your blessings. Ladies and gentlemen, I WELCOME YOU TO LITTLE NIGGA UNIVERSITY.

Oh my, the word "nigger, nigga, niggah, nigggggggaaaaaa, etcetera." no matter how you spell it, it is taboo, isn't it? Throw your opinions about racial slurs and the past out of the window while you are reading this book, and especially this chapter. The word nigga to me means a person who has the qualities of being ignorant, inconsiderate and any other negative impact on the society we live in today. These people of the world attend LNU, and just like any other school, they advertise themselves very well in our communities, schools, televisions, music and especially relationships with their negative little nigga ways.

Let's start off with relationships. What are we getting into relationships for these days? Is it for the companionship? Is it for the sex? Is it because you look good with another good-looking person by your side? LNU has used this to their advantage. They have made people feel as if a great healthy relationship doesn't exist anymore. LNU has put in our minds that it is okay to have sex with multiple partners, and lie to get it. This academy of losers is trying to make it cool to hold double standards above our heads, hearts and brains. LNU is subliminally instilling in our minds that in relationships, sex is the key to making everything work and solving all relationship issues. Being physical is not the big answer, nor is it a major solution. I can suggest a few items that can help with your problems; how about communication, praying about your situations, or just taking responsibility for your actions? I have said this since 2008; intimacy is much better than any sexual intercourse you will ever experience. Later on, we will further examine this statement, but for now let's discuss why LNU needs to be shut down as soon as possible. This school is making sure sex continues to sell throughout our music, movies and other media outlets. No, sex is not bad; but it is not worth you losing your partner, your family or your life. We all love sex, but sex is not what LNU makes it out to be. Ask yourself what sex means to you. I know LNU makes it seem as if it's just sex, but it should be a little deeper than that. If you treat sex as if it's as easy as updating a status on one of the many networking sites, you are putting yourself at risk for sexually transmitted diseases, heartbreak, and maybe danger from a crazy and deranged man or woman who didn't fully understand that it was just sex for you. Sex gets treated too nonchalantly, and I theorize that LNU is one of the main reasons why. If you are going to just have sex, make sure you are safe, and explain to your partner that it's just sex; then they will have the option to take it or leave it.

I am a huge advocate for taking back our society from the LNU mindset. I want to go back into time where a "do you?" letter was the first part of courtship. A "do you?" letter is a little note that asks, "Do you like me? Circle yes or no." LNU has also taken away our "you sleep conversations" where you and the person you are courting fight on who is going to hang up first:

"You hang up, nah you hang up, okay, okay on three we'll both hang up".

LNU has replaced those calls with BlackBerry Messenger, AIM, Facebook chat and text messaging. You cannot get to know someone, or build a relationship via text, emails, or any instant messenger service. It just can't be done! Even with texting, LNU has taken away the sending of random texts throughout the day to see how another person's day is going or to see if they can link up to talk and spend time together. Before LNU leaked their mentally into my society, there was once a time when people weren't prejudged before asking someone out on a date. Some of the fellas can picture what's going on in her mind. If we shut LNU down, we can go back to a time when giving flowers or a card that stated the truth isn't considered a game, and it doesn't scare a woman away. LNU corrupts minds into thinking that just because all men stand up and pee that they are all the same. LNU has made it possible for single men and women to let their past reflect their future. Just because you have failed with relationships in the past does not and I repeat **_does not_** mean you will not eventually fall in love and spread your happiness within a relationship—just have faith. Do not give your past or LNU so much power over you, that it dictates the person you now are. Yes, learn from the past, but be who you are.

A few years ago, I conducted a random questionnaire based on relationships; check out the questions and responses below:

Q: All the men I date seem to expect sex on the first or second date. How long should I wait before becoming intimate with a man?

A: It depends on what you're looking for. If you want to date recreationally and want short-term relationships based on physical attraction and sexual release, you'll probably want to get it on as soon as possible. You'll have the best chance for a long-term, committed relationship if you choose a partner whose vision, value, and belief system is similar to yours. The problem is finding out these things within the first few dates or even the first few months. Once the relationship becomes sexual, sex tends to dominate everything— at least for a while. Sex early on kills true emotional intimacy; this has been my problem in the past, and the only thing you can do is learn from it. You can't reveal your inner selves to each other when you're rolling around under the covers. Having sex with a person you've come to know and like, is usually better than trying to like the person you're having sex with. You can find plenty of people to have sex with. On the other hand, finding a soul mate to share your life with is a lot more difficult. So, how long does it take to really get to know someone? Well, it sure takes more than a few dates. A man or woman who doesn't want to wait for you is telling you, non-verbally, that he or she just wants to be physical. Once the boredom sets in, the lover checks out. Holding out for a few dates is actually a great screening device to separate the players from the real prospects.

Q: How can you tell if someone is really right for you?

A: There are really only two ways. The first way is by being clear about who you are and what you want in a relationship. Mr. or Miss Right is not only the person who pays attention to you. The right person for you is the one who meets your requirements, needs, and wants. These are yours to decide; not friends, parents, or even children—yours alone. It is, after all, your life and your relationship. Secondly, you can test these requirements, needs, and wants by dating many people, because no individual will satisfy all of your specifications. Therefore, if you date several dozen prospects instead of just several, you'll have a greater chance of finding someone who comes closest to fitting your image of the ideal partner. A friend of mine asked me one day, "How can you know what your favorite flavor is, if chocolate is all you've ever tasted?"

Q: What ever happened to just falling in love and forgetting the past, and the rest of bullshit that came with It?

A: People use the words "I love you" so much sometimes, I feel as if the words have lost all meaning. Love isn't supposed to make you feel insecure about yourself or your relationship. Love isn't supposed to make you feel like you're on top of the world and then instantly bring your happy ass down within a matter of hours, if something goes wrong. Love isn't supposed to leave you when you're down and out. Love isn't supposed to drag you along for a ride of abuse, whether verbal or physical. Love isn't supposed to disappear when you feel weak. Love isn't supposed to depart when you say "what you're doing is hurting me and it needs to stop." However, love IS supposed to take you in and embrace you, no matter what you're going through. Love is supposed to hug you when you're having a bad day. Love is supposed to be honest with you, no matter what. Love is supposed to just...love you.

Q: What ever happened to finding someone with your wants and needs and just living your life and being happy?

A: Many people have different wants and needs. Some people want someone to show off like a trophy. Some people want someone to feed their ego occasionally; others want someone to please their every physical need, and some people even use others as a pastime for what they really want.

You don't need to be with anyone to make you happy. Although it's great to have someone to hold you down and to be there, you do not need anyone, I repeat, ANYONE to make you happy. Wants and needs are totally different things. You want someone to be there for you, but you don't need them. You need love and support, but you want it to come from someone who truly loves you.

Q: What ever happened to not caring what other people have to say about your relationship? I see this all the time Steven, and I'm tired of it.

A: When it comes down to it, people are going to talk about you, whether it's in a positive way or a negative way; hell, your own mother will talk about you on the regular. Just keep your head up and keep it pushing, pimping.

Q: What type of affect does sex have on a relationship?

A: No matter what, sex is going to affect your relationship, whether it's positive or negative. Some people say it doesn't matter; those people can kiss my ass and call it a day. It matters! Just as college sex isn't for everyone—some people can do it, some people can't. Some people enjoy sex, and others not so much. Some people need it, while others could just use a "fix" every now and then. People give sex too much power in their relationships also. I must admit, having a partner who matches your sex drive and willingness to create magic and try different things occasionally, would be ideal. However, when you allow it to dictate your feelings towards someone in a relationship, I'd question my motives before moving forward. Sex is strong and it has the potential to be used in all of the wrong ways.

LNU makes relationships seem to be a punishment from God. I hear people say that there is no such thing as a "good man or woman." To me, this comes across as clichéd, and I view it as a cop-out for a man or woman who refuses to look at their own flaws. On those occasions that I do hear men and women give their opinion of a good person, the ideal man seems punkish or from a fantasy, and the woman seems like she is the product of a fairy tale from the 'hood or a music video. This opinion that there are no good men or women out there is overused, crazy and quite boring. Thank you LNU!

Ladies and gentlemen, you get what you ask for, but what are you willing to do to get it? LNU tells you that you should blame each other for why you are unhappy; in reality, it all starts with you!

Little Nigga University encourages parents to neglect their damn kids! If the children are our future, then we need to provide a much better present. I understand that not every relationship will work, but that does not mean you have to shun your parental duties! I know he or she probably cheated, lied or did whatever to make you feel as if you don't want to be in that relationship anymore. Neverthelss, don't cheat the children out of a stable up-bringing because you failed to succeed as a couple. Growing up in a single parent household is no joke, nor is it healthy all of the time. Despite the odds, it can be done, but so can typing with your feet; that doesn't make it acceptable. At the beginning of the book, when I was cursing everyone out I asked, "How would you feel if another person raised your child and did your job?" If you are in this predicament, did you think of an answer? It should make you upset; hell, I'd be furious too. LNU tells you that it's not your fault if the other person in the relationship doesn't want to be around; LNU encourages you to "do you," even if it hurts your little one. The responsibility lies on you to raise a possible future president, or the next sports star, but let's explore this to a greater extent; you have the chance to help raise a person who can help change our society as a doctor, lawyer, teacher or advocate to shut down LNU! Kids are special, but LNU doesn't see it that way. The alumni there feel as if the children's minds are sponges just waiting to absorb the LNU mindset, and they are correct. If we do not take back our homes, LNU will continue to destroy their little minds. For example, have you traveled on public transportation and witnessed the way our youth speak today? It's disgusting, and a damn shame that our kids represent their families like that. I was in high school between the years 1998 through 2002, and as youngster, I had a big mouth that would get me in trouble at least four days out of the week. However, I never publicly showed disrespect when I was with, or even in the presence of, other adults. Honestly, I was no angel; when around my peers, my mouth was worse than Richard Pryor's was. In fact, my whole class-clown persona was based off stand-up comedy routines from Mr. Pryor, Eddie Murphy, or any other comedian I had seen on television. On the other hand, when I faced elders, I knew if it got back to my mother, there would be "smoke in the city." Someone would have to be punished. In my eyes, my mom was the heavyweight champion of ass whooping. There was always a bout when it came to disciplining me; in one corner standing at 5'3, there was a 134 pounds worth of ass whooping woman, with a record of 139-0-3 all by TKO. Hailing from Miami, Florida by way of Boston, Massachusetts, Harriet "Your Ass is Mine" Taylor! Her opponent hiding in the corner standing at 4'7, 79 pounds, when soaking wet, feeling guilty and in trouble, with a record of 0-303 all by TKO, from the land of the bean Boston, Massachusetts. Steven "I Didn't Do It" Barthell! The rounds were very short and always ended the same way. My mom would ask a question, and if I didn't answer it the right way, the one-sided fight began and ended quickly. She struck the fear of God in me and my sister; I suggest the same be done to the children of today. You can't do that by being a weekend parent.

If the relationship didn't work, and you are raising the child or children from different households, just be involved. That means taking him, her or them for more than just the weekend; it will help all parties involved. I know it's easier said than done, but if you don't set up a plan or work out a great way to avoid being a dead beat parent, be prepared for the worse. Take control of your responsibilities and actions; there is no excuse. The child did not ask to be here. I don't know if there is any other reason to want to be there for a child; do not let LNU tell you otherwise. Remember you are a warrior, you are strong, and you are in control at all times. SO, TAKE BACK YOUR HOME.

LNU has made it a non-issue of not leaving the nest—a.k.a. your home. Why do people who are over the age of twenty-five still live at home? In my opinion, there should be no reason you still live at home past that age; unless you have a medical condition, have kids and need help, just finished school and are looking, or you really can't afford it—not knocking you because shit is rough. If you are a grown ass adult who still puts your name on the apple juice, and are not making an effort to leave the nest, you need to be cursed out! Shit happens, and I know that for a fact, but there is no reason to just sit there and wait for big opportunities to happen. Living with the LNU mindset has made you lazy and weak; the funny thing is, the human race is the only one which allows kids to return to the nest. In the wild kingdom, once you are gone, that's it! You are on your own; there is no coming back, because mommy and daddy don't play that shit. Okay, so you have no kids, no job, no education and your mother and father aren't sick. Why the fuck are you still walking around the living room in nothing but tube socks and a tank top; drinking your little nephews last Capri-Sun, watching Sports Center and wondering what's for dinner? This shit has to stop! LNU has you all messed up in the head. Ladies, you are not off the hook because I witness it with you also. Some of you are just hanging around the house doing hair all damn day watching, *Maury: You are Not the Father*, and won't even pick up a damn broom to make sure the house is clean. You have three bad kids, who need their asses beat, running amuck on your block; you wonder why they aren't learning a damn thing in school, but feel as if people owe you something. Oh, hell naw! Get the hell up, work, provide and move the fuck out please. This LNU mentality has the game twisted, like monkeys wearing wedding dresses to a funeral.

As I mentioned before, shit happens, and people run into tough and hard times; but "got damn." It isn't cool, if it's been a few years, and you are still at home with no excuses. I don't expect everyone to be out of their parents' house at a young age like me, (nineteen and I pray I never go back), but something has to give. It is time to re-evaluate your goals and your motives in life. It is time to get out from under the influence of LNU and grow up.

This school, Little Nigga University, needs to be shut down immediately. Earlier in the chapter we talked about sex and I stated, "If you are going to just have sex make sure you are safe and explain to your partner that it's just sex; then they have the choice of taking it or leaving it." I know for a fact many people disagreed with me when

I said intimacy is better than sex. I understand that a relationship isn't for everyone, even though I disagree that things should be this way; but if you are going to participate in sexual intercourse, make sure you are doing it correctly, especially by protecting yourselves. LNU has made a point to create liars when it comes to sex and other physical activities. I'm tired of every male advertising like they have the best sex game in the world. Fellas, let's be honest. You're not a porn star or even a porn star's stunt double. Start off the relationship by being honest with these women, so they will know what they're getting themselves into. This isn't 1998, when most people my age were freshmen in high school, and the closest thing we got to the female vagina was watching late night cable television. I am going to need my fellas to stop fronting as if they don't go down on women. There is nothing wrong with it, in my opinion. However, I know that everyone cannot receive oral sex, if it's sloppy, or if she's not worth it. If you do not know if she's worth it, then you shouldn't be having sex with her in the first place. Stop looking to "get yours." Is that really your only goal in having sex? One of the main goals in having sex is to stimulate the female clitoris as many times as possible during the "session." There are no limits; if you are going to have sex, then why hold back? Take your time, practice, take your time, practice, take your damn time, and practice. These women trust you with their bodies, you're taking advantage in all the wrong ways, and this is not okay. I know LNU has taught you that being selfish is the right way to go, but obviously most women would disagree. Some of you are getting into bed, messing up, then are left wondering why they ran to someone else. Them leaving may bea cop-out, but it's reality. Don't become the fella around the way that knows how to "slop the rug and not beat up the pillow". Come on, get it together; there should be no reason why your new nickname becomes "EATbox" and "FLOPsteady."

Ladies, I love each and every one of you with all of my heart, but LNU has some of you messing up in the bedroom as well. Words of advice: don't just lay there and wait for the action to happen. Oral sex is the "in" thing. I'm going to be real bold, and tell you to suck your man's penis, because if you don't, there will be another woman who is willing to do so and not complain. Furthermore, before you expect a man to perform oral sex, or as a good friend of mine tweets on Twitter, "conduct in the orals," make sure your vagina is clean. I've heard stories about brothers having "coco bread" all over their mouths from a terrible yeast infection, or catching terrible nasty diseases from a contaminated vagina. There is the douche, soap, and etcetera. My uncle once said "Woman, wash yourself please! Flop flop, fizz fizz; oh what a relief it is." In other words, clean the streets before we travel downtown please. Just as I told the guys, why hold back? You are already having sex! This is the route you have chosen, so protect yourself and do not have sex just for the fun of it. LNU has made it possible to live in a world where not living up to double standards are a deal breaker. I personally feel that being intimate with one person is the thing to do, but in the past, I have had the mentality of not wanting to waste anyone's time with the idea of being in a relationship; I thought having recreational sex was okay and it was your God given right to do as you please.

Welcome to Little Nigga University everyone; a "school" with a mindset that is poisoning our society with bad parenting, bad relationships, bad living habits and bad sex. LNU classes make it possible to take away all of our morals and goals. There was once a time when going to the corner store didn't involve having to worry about being stuck in the middle of a cross fire, or witnessing a drug deal. I remember when the only issue I had with the opposite sex was if I had the cooties and not an STD. I can't pretend that violence, drugs, dead beat parents and bad relationships are new issues; but I can tell you that this LNU mindset, which plagues our society, is increasing them. Therefore, unless we take control and shut this school down, we will perish. It's not going to happen overnight, and it's going to take more than a group or team. It's going to take all of us to shut it down. Once we put our pride aside, focus on the bigger issues of life, and stop complaining on how fucked up things are, we will move forward. I believe in the old saying, if you are not the solution then you are increasing the problem. Instead of simply pointing out LNU's methods, we need to help guide the students of this mindset to a much brighter future and way of life. We cannot expect to have peace or a drug-free world by only talking about it; let's get together and solve it. How can you comment on someone's parenting skills if you are not willing to help improve them? How can we create jokes about someone still living at home, if we aren't assisting in solving their plight? Without helping, we increase funding to keep the school of ignorance, hate, selfishness and the ability to move backwards in life open. Welcome. To. Little. Nigga. University!

Dear ,

Hey; how is it going? I was thinking about you earlier and instead of calling you, I decided to write you a letter. I just wanted to thank you for being you in every way. I get so excited when I get out of bed and think of you. I enjoyed the moment that we shared when we had our first date. I remember it like it was yesterday; you came by the house. I fixed my baked ziti with Italian sausages; we listened to the new Brian McKnight c.d., and just enjoyed each other's company. I got a kick out of running through the rain holding hands, stopping in the middle of the downpour, and I gazing into your eyes. It was then that I knew I was in front of someone special. That is when we shared our first kiss. I can still feel the wetness on your face, as your lips touched mine. You can say it was the first of many great moments with the person who I want to spend the rest of my life with.

Do you remember when you accidentally bleached my University of Miami sweatshirt? At first, I was pissed. Eventually, I got over it and apologized for raising my voice. What about the time we met each other's parents? Both of us were nervous as all hell, but together we got through it. Now that I think about it, our mothers knew each other from high school, and they wouldn't shut up about it. Through the time that we have spent together, I am proud to say that I respect how you carry yourself around our friends, family, and in public. Oh, before I forget, the best crew in the world says hi. Each day we get more and more awesome—okay enough about my friends. Anyway, I miss you. I really, really miss you. I miss the way you wake me up when I don't hear my alarm in the morning. I miss the way your eyes light up when you see me; sometimes the feeling is as if we are seeing each other for the very first time. I miss the way your nose flares out when u get mad. The way you start talking really fast, and I have to slow you down to understand your anger. I miss the fact that during the summer we can root for the same baseball team, but during the basketball and football seasons, become sports enemies. Even though my love for you is stronger, my love for team 305 is deep!

I can't ever forget that first night you spent at my house and me at yours; how amazed you looked when I agreed that we should wait for us to make love until we were both ready to take that next step. When it did happen, it was the best reward for waiting. Even with all the things we have in common, there were a couple of bad times, like you saying Kobe is better than D-Wade (BULLSHIT!). Seriously, there were bad times, such as when you would get annoyed when I repeated the words of our favorite movies, or the way you snored at night, and to this day you claim you don't, even after I recorded you. As a matter of fact, now that I think about it, every problem that we have went through with one another was settled right then and there. I really respect that when you aren't feeling something I do, or was doing, you will voice and have voiced your opinion on it; you didn't complain to our friends or anyone else. You came to me, and I did the same thing. I love that about you. I can never ever forget when you took off of work early that day when I was as sick as a dog, and tended to my every little need, even though I acted like a big baby.

You don't trip when I chill with my friends, both male and female. I even learned that when you party without me, you dance alone—you represent me. I am proud to say, I finally found someone who I can trust with no doubt in my mind. I think my uncles are still pissed about us running them off the table when playing spades at my grandmother's house. By the way, she's so in love with you; I think she loves you more than I do. I also can't forget those times when we attended your church one Sunday, and my church the next Sunday.

For the first time in my life, I have the confidence to not worry about me or you growing apart from each other, and I appreciate you in every way. Thru the good times and the bad times, it's a pleasure to have you in my life and an honor to say I love you.

With Much Love,

Steven

P.S. It's just too bad you don't exist.

Even though you are not here, my heart and my faith in God tells me He's sending you really soon. I love you, and I thank you in advance.

MY CITY

I once lived in a city. It was a strong, safe city. It had high walls around it, built in earlier times to fend off frequent attackers. The walls were strong ones, and I maintained them in order to keep myself safe from hurtful things. I can't say I felt safe in my strong city, but it was as close as I could get. However, I was alone in my city. My city had become a prison for me. The same walls which I had built to keep out pain had also kept out good things, like the things that make life worth living. While I was relatively safe in my city, I was besieged in a prison of my own making. Yet, I continued maintenance on my walls. I chose the safety of a prison rather than face the dangers that lay on the outside.

Even after there were no more attacks, and no more attackers, I kept up my city's walls. Then one day, I heard of another city, from a traveler, who had gained my trust. I gave her admittance to my city. It was the first real company I had had in a very long time. Time after time, my traveler friend returned. I soon began to lose interest in my walls. It's amazing how fast they fell when I forgot about them. I don't know if my traveler friend thought it strange to find the walls around my city coming down, but I did not notice. I enjoyed her company so much that my walls did not even cross my mind. I wondered what sort of city it was that my traveler friend hailed from.

It was then that I realized that my walls had completely fallen. They were beyond repair, but I did not wish to build them up again. So, I left my once strong city and set out to find that other city from whence my traveler friend had come. The place where I, for some reason, had begun to believe I could be safe and yet not alone. It was not a long journey, and I soon reached the city I was looking for. I don't know what I expected to see when I reached that city, but what a sinking feeling I had when I stood before the city and found it surrounded by high walls, probably as strong and solid as mine had once been. I could not get in, but I could not go back, for the old city could not ever be home again.

So now I wander outside of the other city. I still talk to my traveler friend, and I try to glean, from the things she says, what the city must be like. Oh, how I long to be in that city. To have the walls open their gates for me. To have a city to call home once more and hopefully be better off than I was before. I know what I left behind; I do not miss it, nor do I feel the least bit of longing to return. Therefore, I wait on the outside of this other city praying that someday I can win admittance. Although, I fear I may have to wait forever.

COURT, LEARN, LOVE, MARRY

W hat are our motives for being in a relationship? Is it for the sex? Is it to look good with each other, or is it to merely waste our time? In committed relationships, the goal and the motives should be the following:

1.   Courtship
2.   Learning each other
3.   Loving each other and then marrying each other

If you do not want to be in a commitment then just continue fucking each other. Relationships should be deeper than chilling and having sex, and this applies to men and women.

Life is about growth; we are supposed to try to reach our full potential, and try to touch the stars. Well, we're supposed to do the same in relationships. I have grown over time, and learned that it isn't just a woman that I want in my life. I also want a connection, intimacy, and SECURITY! When I was 18, it was just about having sex; at age 21, sex and more sex and now that I am 26, I should need and want more than that. We need to be able to stimulate someone's mind and not just their body. I want my woman to be able to look at me and say to herself, "Damn I love him," without me even touching her. I want my whisper to be able to intrigue her heart and make her know that she has something good. Hell, it could be the smell of my cologne or the type of soap I use that makes her go crazy. It's amazing what love can do to a person, because with a connection, intimacy, and security you get more from the relationship than you would with someone you're only fucking or cuddling.

The sad thing is, some people don't even know what courtship is. They haven't even been on a real date, or ever been courted. It all goes back to that LNU mentality of ignorance and the unwillingness to open up your mind and heart. Men, courtship is actually working hard at trying to date a woman. It's about showing her that you are the man that you claim to be; it's not just about flowers and candy, but being creative. Take her out on a picnic; the movies are only good during the middle of a courtship. Go out for a walk and talk, because going out to eat just isn't cutting it anymore! Courtship is almost like a tryout; there is an application process and rules for dating. If a commitment is not what you are looking for, then I suggest you return back to LNU; just don't bother communicating on that level with the opposite sex or same sex. (To each his or her own; no judgment from me I'm just a man who writes.) Courtship is supposed to be fun, even though I did mention an application process, which is only a metaphor. The application process is used so you won't have any surprises in the future. We will explore this concept further in the chapter "Joys & Pains." In the meantime, here is an example of my dating application:

Applicant Information:

Applicant Name: _____

Home Phone: _____

Other Contact #: _____

Email Address: _____

Current Address:
    Number and street: _____
    City: _____
    State and Zip: _____

How were you referred?:_____

Employment position(s) applying for:_____

Are you applying for:

Temporary? (booty call or transitional relationship) [ ] Y or [ ] N

Regular full-time work? [ ] Y or [ ] N

What days and hours are you available to spend quality time?
_____

If applying for temporary work, when will you be available?
_____

On what date can you start? __ / __ / __

Can you do weekends? [ ] Y or [ ] N

Can you do evenings, i.e.,spend the night and actually want to?
[ ] Y or [ ] N

Are you available to put in overtime, so eventually I won't have to
look for other applicants? [ ] Y or [ ] N

Personal Information:

Have you ever cheated before? [ ] Y or [ ] N

If yes, please explain (include dates): _____

Do you have any friends, relatives, or acquaintances that know me?
[ ] Y or [ ] N

If yes, state name and relationship: _____

If chosen, do you have the means to come see me? [ ] Y or [ ] N

Are you over the age of 18? (If you look under 18, I am required to
look at verification of minimum state legal age.) [ ] Y or [ ] N

If chosen, would you be able to present evidence of your U.S. citizenship or proof of your legal right to live in the United States? [ ] Y or [ ] N

Are you able to perform the essential functions of being with me, either with or without reasonable accommodations? (Ex: the bedroom, for which you are applying.) [ ] Y or [ ] N

If no, describe the functions that cannot be performed; i.e., what are you not willing to do?
_____

Do you have any children? [] Y or [] N
If so, how many?_____

Do you take care of them? [] Y or [] N _____
(Note: If no, NO NEED TO CONTINUE FROM THIS POINT.)

If you have multiple children, how many mothers or fathers are there?

Is the mother or father of your child or children CRAZY? [] Y [] N
(Note: If yes, then NO NEED TO APPLY.)

Have you ever been convicted of a criminal offense (felony or misdemeanor)? [ ] Y or [ ] N

If yes, please list the state where the crime occurred, the nature of the crime(s), when and where convicted and disposition of the case._____

*** (Note: If you are currently locked up or have open cases, your application will not be reviewed. That includes DV (Domestic Violence) Drugs, Alcohol Problems and Bad Tempers.

Education:

High School:_____
College:_____

Vocational (Nail/Barber School):_____
Number of years completed: _____
Did you graduate? [ ] Y or [ ] N
Degree/diploma earned: _____

Employment History:

Are you currently employed? [ ] Y or [ ] N
If you are currently employed, may we contact your current employer to verify this? [ ] Y or [ ] N

Name of Employer:_____
Name of Supervisor:_____
Telephone Number:_____
Business Type: _____
Address:_____
City, state, zip:_____

Length of Employment (Include Dates): _____
Position and Duties:_____

References:

List three people below who have knowledge of your work performance within the last four years. Please include professional references only. Ex: past girlfriends, boyfriends, wives, husbands. booty calls, etc.

Name: First and last: _____
Telephone Number:_____
Address:_____
City, state, zip:_____
Occupation: _____
Number of Years Acquainted: _____

Name: First and last: _____
Telephone Number:_____
Address:_____
City, state, zip:_____
Occupation: _____

Number of Years Acquainted: _____

Name: First and last: _____
Telephone Number:_____
Address:_____
City, state, zip:_____
Occupation: _____
Number of Years Acquainted: _____

Relationship History:

Are you currently taken??? [ ] Y or [ ] N

If you are currently taken, may we contact your current girl or boyfriend to verify this, and then snitch? [ ] Y or [ ] N

***Please Read and Initial Each Paragraph, and Sign Below.

I certify that I have not purposely withheld any information that might adversely affect my chances for being in this relationship. I attest to the fact that the answers given by me are true and correct to the best of my knowledge and ability. I understand that any omission (including any misstatement) of material fact on this application or on any document used to secure this position can be grounds for rejection of application or, if I am chosen, terms for my immediate expulsion. ____

I understand that if I am chosen, my new relationship status is for the long haul and is not just a rebound thing. ____

I permit you to examine my relationship history, references, record of employment, education record, and any other information I have provided. I also state that my last relationship is in the past and I will never bring it up. ____

By signing this application, you also verify the following:

1. I am True to Myself.
2. I am honest.
3. I show affection, and will let you know that I'm not leaving.
4. I'm willing to be your best friend, and communicate well.
5. I know what I want out of the relationship.
6. I will accept you for you or resign.
7. You will never have to worry about me cheating or lying.
8. You will never have to worry about our bedroom activities because they will always be fresh and spicy.
9. You will never have to worry about having "me" time.
10. You will never have to worry about reviewing another application after this one.

The application is all a mental thing; if you take good mental notes, you really should have nothing to worry about. If you are doing your part in a relationship and the other person doesn't comply, tell him or her SEEFUCKYALATA.

There are rules for dating. Yes, there are do's and don'ts. Everyone needs a plan, although some work better than others. Check this out:

Dating Do's:

* Be attentive to your date. When faced with the dilemma of whether to tell all or listen attentively, many singles prefer to listen. Tara is a 22-year-old college student who feels she has the role of "listener". "If you listen to your date, they think you're interesting, even though you haven't actually said anything. Just keep asking questions and they'll think you're brilliant and fascinating." Good point T; everyone wants to feel important, and sometimes having a good ear to listen helps. However, be careful and don't tell your date everything! We'll get to that a little later.

* Maintain eye contact. Just make sure it's not too intense. Remember, you aren't a hawk eyeballing its prey. I've learned while growing up that creating eye contact helps a person respect you more. Time and time again you'll get some irrational person who might say "why are you looking at me like that?" They may be

paranoid because some people love to lie, and are afraid you'll see right through them.

* Plan your date out ahead of time. Avoid falling into the vicious cycle of saying, "I don't know, what do you want to do?" Decide on something and do it. Be open to other suggestions if your plans don't work out.

* Meet in a public place on your first date. Not only is this a safe idea, it also allows for distractions, should conversation lag. Al, my former barber, 34, agrees: "Leave the one-on-one romantic dates for when you really feel you are into a person." Do something different for a change; like ice skating, going to the zoo, picnicking, etcetera. You can't take every date to TGI Fridays, can you?

* Offer to split the bill; the issue of who pays is probably one of the largest sources of confusion for singles. Most people today feel that the bill is the responsibility of the person that asked for the date, and although most may agree with this, it is still courteous to offer to pay half. You should always be prepared to split the costs, in any case. If your date does pick up the tab, offer to pay the next time. Sometimes this is the most awkward part of the date, but personally, I don't go on dates unless I'm prepared to pay. That mentality is a southern gentleman thing, I suppose.

* Act chivalrous or mannerly. Men, the woman's liberation movement may have provided women with the means to financial independence and positions of power, but being liberated does not mean that a woman no longer appreciates those little things that make you a gentleman. Open doors for your date; pull out her chair for her, and make sure she gets home safely. These things make a good impression. Samantha, a 23 year-old close friend of mine, believes that, "If used correctly, chivalry is the charm of all charms; if overused, it seems like machismo." Sam may be right; so long as a guy knows when to pick the right situation to be gentlemanly, he's good to go.

* Follow-up with your date, by calling or emailing him or her to let them know you had a good time. However, be careful not to let this come across as a plea to see them again right away. Acknowledging

your enjoyment of the date is simply a courtesy. If your date had an enjoyable time too, that will only be icing on the cake! It may even signify that more dates are in your future. It's just the appropriate thing to do; especially if a brother is looking for that special someone.

* Be humorous; not only will this put your date at ease, it will also show them you have a sense of humor. After all, there is no reason why your date should feel like they are at work or attending a board meeting. Just loosen up and have fun.

* Discuss heavier topics, if the atmosphere is right. Let's face it; some people SHOULD stick to small talk, but if you're informed on a topic, go ahead and discuss it. This would be a good time to discern what your date considers appropriate and prohibited. It is better to be informed about this early on. If you aren't versed on a topic, shut the fuck up about it, and continue talking about something else. Nobody likes a smart dumb person.

Dating Don'ts:

* Don't get distracted during a date. Turn off your cell phone, put it on silent, or set it to vibrate; understandably, this may not apply to people with kids. Also keep your eyes from wandering. Nothing shows a greater lack of interest or respect on your part, than fielding phone calls and checking out the staff in the restaurant. This applies to men and women.

* Don't turn your date into a therapy session; avoid subjects like past significant others, a bad relationship with your mother, or your growing sense of concern over the strange growth you've discovered on your back. A date is the time to get to know a potential love interest. Those being said, save the session for your therapist.

* Don't be arrogant, overconfident or conceited. No one is perfect, thus nothing is more annoying than someone who acts like they are. I know I can appear to be overconfident ALL THE DAMN TIME, but it isn't true. You have to humble yourself occasionally.

* Don't agree for the sake of agreeing, because it's important to stand your ground on certain topics. The point of dating is to get to

know one another. However, it is okay to enjoy an intellectual debate, as long as you avoid insulting your date's intelligence, and their pride.

* Don't try to make any uninvited physical advances. There are so many different opinions on what is physically acceptable on a date. Ciarra, aged 28, holds the opinion that if there is chemistry, the physical aspects of a relationship will fall into place. "If things feel right, then hold hands, kiss; whatever feels right. Nothing is worse, though, than a first date...[that shows too much] PDA (public displays of affection). It's sort of like they are staking their claim, which is a major turn-off." I agree you should let things flow, and if anything happens outside of the occasional dinner and movie, just go with it; that's only if both parties want things to go that way. Remember you're in control of your actions and feelings at all times.

* LADIES! Don't be afraid to ask a man for a date. In fact, many men find women, who make the first move, attractive and confident. Twenty-four year old Katie agrees: "A woman asking a man for a date doesn't have to be a pathetic plea to listen to John Legend over a candlelit dinner. You can invite the guy to something you are going to anyway, like a concert, so it's like you are asking them to come along." I also agree with this opinion; I personally think that if a woman knows what she wants, then she should go get it. However, this can also be a bad thing, according to Mike, who is also 24. He says, "Sometimes I like the more traditional approach, like me asking her out to dinner and maybe a walk on the beach. I don't know; maybe it's my ego or something." Well, Mike, maybe it's just me but I LOVE AN AGGRESSIVE WOMAN, man! Nothing is sexier.

* Don't consume large amounts of alcohol. During my younger days, I watched an Arnold Schwarzenegger movie, and he told his intoxicated wife, "You should not drink and bake." Well, the same holds true for dating; you should not drink and date. Although the reasons for this are obvious, drinking is a trap many people fall into, which subsequently ruins many people's chances for a second date. If you must drink, stick with one beer or a single glass of wine. No questions! Drinking can lead you down the wrong path; trust me, I'm a witness.

* Don't be afraid to end the date early. If things are not working out, or you are uncomfortable, feel free to end the date at any time. Seefuckyalata means seefuckyalata. Why waste your time, or their time?

You can agree or you can disagree, but in the dating arena, you have to follow some type of guidelines. So, just like everything else I write, feel free to debate whether the "The Rules" are right or wrong for your life.

In relationships, most do not ask many questions. However, many assumptions are made; this causes a lot of us to think we know how the opposite sex's mind works. This forfeits the process of understanding each other. We throw around the words, "I love you" so much, they become as common as "good morning, good afternoon, and goodnight." Learning is fundamental; it gives you a chance to educate yourself on the inner mechanics of someone's mind without prejudging. There is no way to get to know someone without communicating with him or her. We discussed this earlier; what you should be doing is trying to spend as much time with the person and figuring out if this is something you can do for a while. Most of us get into relationships and use people as a transition to something better, or treat them as if they are a temporary worker. In the real world, this behavior does not cut it. I was once a firm believer in dating around and having sex occasionally. I no longer believe in that practice, but that's just me. Being in a commitment will open up your eyes to new experiences and also give you a chance to avoid selling yourself short. Just to reiterate, if you are not the commitment type, this chapter is definitely not for you! If you are in a relationship and haven't learned much about your significant other, I would began an inquiry as soon as possible. You may ask things such as, what are their dreams? How strong is their faith? Do they want children? If they already have children, do they want more? Do they plan to get married in the future? The deeper the relationship becomes, the deeper the questions should be. You may consider asking things like, are you in debt? How much do you owe? This line of questioning may seem strange, but once a ring is on your finger, the debt is no longer solely his or her debt—it's "our debt". Learning is the key to realizing if you can or cannot spend your time, money and love on someone. Learn to learn! You may be quite surprised at the answers you get.

Sometimes the learning process will determine how long the relationship lasts, and if it's worth the fight.

Love and marriage are treated like forbidden words in today's society. If I mention either one, people around me go crazy! Love and marriage are not diseases and don't require cures. I've heard people say, "Oh my gosh, love is in the air; time to grab my face mask" Huh? What? What the fuck? Is this how the world's strongest feeling should be treated? I think we need to start re-evaluating our thoughts on love. I know you may have been hurt before, and believe you have seen and heard it all. I was one of those people who had a wall over my heart too. The poem before the chapter tells it all. Read "My City" all over again and come back to this point. I have learned to love again; it all started with the person in my reflection, but I have gotten over the past. I suggest you do the same. With love, you cannot allow your past to reflect your future; you can only learn from it and move on. How do we love each other? Well, it's more than just a physical thing, although it is mistaken for lust all the damn time. As I mentioned before, love is about finding a new experience with someone you never thought you'd meet; someone who turns your life around completely, it's not a weekend or temporary thing.

So what are your motives in a relationship? If courting someone, learning him or her, loving him or her and then eventually marrying him or her doesn't work, what are you going to do? Are you going to give up? Are you going to risk becoming a victim of bitterness and loneliness? Dating multiple people forever will only soothe your soul temporarily, and won't solve any of your problems. Marriage to me is a way to present each other to God and make your union solid; it's a form of security, and a method to help you get into heaven, if you are in a relationship. Marriage is deep; it is a partnership, not a business. People need to stop getting married for all of the wrong reasons. Yes, I know you want to keep your family together; yes, you want to continue to look good in front of people. However, if you are not happy in your relationship before marriage, a ring on your finger isn't going to change that. If you are not praying for a stronger relationship, and to keep the flame going, you will fail. We will explore marriage and maintaining a relationship in the later chapters.

Courting, Learning, Loving and Marriage is the path I'm paving, and I challenge you to do the same. Be aware that this strategy only helps with commitments; if you are not ready or do not know what you want, then take more time to learn and love yourself. It will make things so much easier.

MY LIFE (PART I)

Time and time again life will knock you down-it may even knock you out. Nevertheless, you have to fight within yourself to make the count before you are deemed finished by the referee; in the case of humans in real life, this would mean being counted out by your own society. There is an inner warrior in each one of us, so we have to dig deep to unleash that beast in order to overcome the hardships and struggles. Life throws curve balls every once in a while; and just like in baseball, where most batters struggle with making contact, sometimes you will have a hard time "making contact" in life. However, instead of giving up, work harder so it can be one less battle to fight later. You are a conqueror. You are a survivor. You are a warrior, who is capable of changing the world. We were put on this earth to fight; not just physical battles, but also mental, spiritual, and subconscious battles. We weren't given the ability to breath, or the honor to walk, just to sit around worrying about shit we can't handle, or things we have no control over. How strong are you? Are you capable of hitting rock bottom and then climbing up? Are you going to let hardships overcome you? No, you are not! At least you shouldn't. You are stronger than you know; you are capable of climbing the highest mountains and rising from the hardest falls. No more being sympathetic towards your situations, and no more being afraid of failure. If you want sympathy, get the nearest dictionary and look between shit and syphilis. We forget that before we win, we must learn how to lose. You may ask, "Why Steven? Why lose when we can win at all times?" Well, the meaning behind that saying is, you should be prepared at all times for any and everything. Furthermore, in business, there's a saying that states, "You might take a loss before gaining any type of profit." I am going to use myself as an example in this chapter. Yes, we are about to delve into the life of Steven Antwain Barthell, just to show you that you are a champion and that if I can learn, grow and continue to learn and grow you can too. I do warn you if you are close, or have ever been close to me, it might shock you that I am not perfect and I have made some mistakes. I will tell you things that might make you think back and say to yourself, "Oh now I see." This chapter includes a brief description of my life, as seen through my eyes. Therefore, by no means am I trying to strike controversy; neither will I falsely accuse anybody of what happened between 1984 and 2010. Let's dig deeper into my relationships, my passion for basketball and music, and learn how I became the person I am now.

As a child, a teen and a young adult, I had my share of hardships. I grew up in a mostly one parent household; I did have a stepfather momentarily, but just like with many relationships, it didn't last between him and my mother. My father was never there, and to my knowledge never wanted to be there. My mom did her best raising my sister and me, but I could tell it wasn't easy. From my birth to the age of 12 or 13, I thought life was simple and easy. During the first four years of my existence, I was spoiled rotten by love, because I was the first grandson of my generation maternally and paternally. I was also adorable (as I laugh to myself at that last description). My baby sister, Jannell, who has grown to be an intelligent, beautiful, yet aggravating, annoying, and strong young woman, came in 1988. This changed my whole life; from sharing toys to sharing my mother's affection. This was very hard on a boy my age, and although we were equally loved, between the ages of four and 12, I didn't see it that way. I would get jealous over things I couldn't control, and get upset over not having the two parents my sister had in one house. It would upset me that Jannell's grandparents and other family members from her paternal side would shower her with extra gifts, time and love. Being the only boy for maybe fifteen years, on the maternal side, affected me negatively as a kid. Surrounded by four girls, and not knowing what it felt like to have a real father around also hurt. My mother and stepfather separated when I was 10 or 11, and up until the separation, the holiday's, birthdays and other celebrations were always top notch. We had everything children could ask for, from clothes to toys. We had a great support system when we had troubles in school, or with other peers, but all of this changed once they divorced. I felt like it was my fault for being a bad child, and this affected my studies, my behavior in elementary school, and my relationship with my sister, stepbrother and cousins. I began to demand attention by lashing out verbally on teachers, adult figures and even my mother; I once told her I hated her during a family trip.

Moving to different cities or towns didn't help either. I suppose moving was my mom's way of escaping all the madness, or maybe her way to start over. While living in Springfield, Massachusetts, I once got suspended from school for abusing a teacher with my venomous tongue; I called him a racist and called him every name in the book, thinking this would get me sent back to Boston where I had spent so many years with friends and family. However, I didn't exactly get the attention I expected; I was suspended for three days, received an ass whooping from my mother, which was her form of punishment until I got older, and I was forced to talk to a guidance counselor. That didn't help much because the guidance counselor was more interested in finding out if my mother was dating anyone, than trying to analyze the shit I was going through.

Not only was my behavior changing, but my body was changing, and I didn't know how to react or handle the transformation. There was no man to teach me about sports, or puberty. No one to explain to me why I would get an erection at the sight of the pretty girls who were in school, on television, in magazines, or even at a bus stop. Our financial situation was also shifting; we went from having a two-income household, to my mother losing her job. This resulted in her struggling to keep food in our mouth's and a roof over our head. She could have resumed a relationship with someone she wasn't happy with, but I suppose her pride wouldn't allow her to. I didn't know all of the details of why my parents broke up; this left me confused and bewildered as I tried to comprehend the reality that there were only three instead of four, while traveling from Massachusetts to the state of Florida.

When we initially relocated, we lived in a small town called Lake Wales. My sister and I have very light complexions, but everyone in Lake Wales was darker and bigger—much bigger—than we were. We definitely stood out from our other family members and the general population. My sister and I were also very outstanding when it came to our studies, and we were always on the Honor Roll. (Well, she was on it more than I, because of my mouth and class clown attitude, or ass clown attitude, as my great-grandmother called it, after I fought like an idiot over a bad joke told in science class one day). We were called nerds or weirdoes, and since our skin was lighter than most Black people around us, we were called "crackers," a Caucasian racial slur. We still received love from our family members; especially my late uncles Willy and Billy Joe. No love was withheld from my late great-grandmother and lovely Aunt Rosie either; my aunt taught me that if I didn't stick up for myself, I would be walked over, and I am grateful for that knowledge. I also have my cousins to thank for introducing me to self-confidence in my talents. My mom never hesitated to let her children know, "I'm the boss, you're the child. You will do as I say, or be on your own." She exhibited strong tough love; it was a little too tough, sometimes to the point of being overbearing. I know she wasn't trying to fail, but if she were to reflect on the past, I'm sure she would have chosen to do some things differently. On the other hand, knowing her, she probably wouldn't have had it any other way. I suppose that's where my resiliency and my "put it into God's hands" attitude stems from. My mother made sure we had God in our lives and that we knew He was the greater power. Upon moving down to Florida,I realized that just because a person's blood flows through your veins, that fact doesn't make the person family.

Although we were allowed to stay with family upon arrival to Florida, my mom knew we needed our own place. So, we eventually moved to Miami. Everyone knows I love the city of Miami, and I represent every sports team they have, including the Miami Heat, Dolphins and Hurricanes. However, what most may not know is, I hated it there while I lived there. Everyone knew everyone, and if you didn't play sports, you were a sissy or a nerd. Furthermore, what some people don't know about Miami is, if you don't have a home, job security, or a dependable income, you will struggle ten times more than you will in other cities, because Miami is a very expensive city to survive in with no wages. My mother never had a problem obtaining a job; however, the economy made it difficult to keep one. I found myself unable to do most things my peers did, unless I earned a little money on my own. Therefore, I started tutoring a neighbor on her math and English studies. It didn't hurt that I was good friends with her brother, although it could also be a bad thing because it was easy to get distracted with video games and wrestling. Due to this friendship, sports would become important in my life soon after.

The living arrangements didn't last for both me and my sister, because my mom eventually sent my sister back to Massachusetts to live with her father and grandfather, which left my mother and me. My sister was now back in Boston, which fucked me up. I would say to myself at night, "why not me too?" or "why the fuck should I struggle too? This isn't my fault." I definitely wasn't being a team player for my mom, who needed me as a crutch and as motivation to keep pushing and fighting.

My first year of high school in Miami taught me that you have to fight for what you want, or someone else will swoop in and take it. I was a freshman in high school now, full of confidence and I started to notice I was now attractive to the opposite sex. I also discovered that the women in high school were like nothing I had ever seen in my life. Even though they ranged from the ages of 15-19, these girls carried themselves as if they were grown, by having their own cars, and the bodies of women older than 22. Consequently, I gained a plethora of crushes. I've always been cute, but in my eighth and ninth grade years, I became more than cute, and I would flirt my ass off. I met my first crush in Miami. She lived around the corner from me. I ruined that relationship because of my immaturity, and choosing to play sports over getting to know her. She was also my first kiss; well, sort of; someone actually dared her to kiss me in front of her friends. I was playing a three-on-three basketball game with some friends; she came up to me during a break, and laid one the best kisses I have ever had in my life on me. My seven-year old cousin Tony jumped over the fence with no hands, to run into our house and yell that I kissed her. Later on, my aunt sat me down and explained the consequences of dealing with the female species; she also told me not to do things in front of the younger kids. Of course, as a 15-year-old boy, I thought I knew everything, and I brushed the advice off. The proof that I didn't know it all rested in my future issues with women, as I got older. After that kiss, I thought I was the "man" until I found out she was only interested for maybe a month or two. I eventually had my first sexual experience also, which is something I would have postponed if I had had the knowledge I have now.

Because I was too young to work, and because my mother's earnings were spent on rent, bills and food, I couldn't really experience the true Miami life as a young teen. School was no different; I still gained great grades, but my mouth continued to get me into trouble. Sports, especially basketball became a motivational tool for me. As a third grader, I fell in love with basketball as I watched Scottie Pippen dish the ball to Michael Jordan on television; Pippen was and always will be my favorite player of all time. I would practice and practice my game, and my skills would improve every year. With this improvement, my knowledge and respect for the game grew also.

I remember trying out for my first team in Miami; I will never forget the hard work I put in during the previous summer to try and become a team player for the Miami Norland Senior High School Vikings. I was determined to prove to the neighborhood that I was more than just good around them, so I tried out for the varsity team. (Now everyone knows if you play varsity sports in the state of Florida, or in the city of Miami, you have connections, or you are a prodigal child of a great athlete). I had neither of these going for me, and I failed tremendously. I shot the ball very well, but my footwork was terrible and my defense was worse. I was cut the very first day; I didn't bother trying out for junior varsity, because my pride and ego were crushed. However, I wanted to play so bad. I eventually tried out for the optimism league and made the team as a starter, because I told the coach where I was comfortable playing. However, my hoop dreams would ultimately come to an end, because I opened my mouth and let my popularity make me egotistical.

I found one of my niches in a class I almost dropped. It was my speech and debate class; after the first day, I never wanted to speak again. My teacher, Ms. Lori Bailey, was a member of the famous sorority, Alpha Kappa Alpha, Inc., and I will never forget her. She told me I had the gift of gab and that I should practice in front of the mirror and in front of my little cousins, or she was going to fail me. I had never failed a class in my life; my mother thought it strange that I didn't initially do well in this class, because I was always trying to perform in front of my family members during the holiday's and while in the house. I was always a talkative child and didn't know when to shut the hell up, according to my aunt Bara. However, I had never written anything or made a speech in front of my peers; except for singing in my third grade talent show, where I won fourth place. (I wonder if the kids who did "At the Playground" are still singers.)

Anyway, I studied, and the more I practiced speaking, the better I became. My method to get through a speech was to pretend that no one else was in the room, and I was the president of the United States. I also started learning the art of throwing in humor during my speeches, while debating with classmates. Humor is music without the melody to me; it's a way to make someone smile or feel good. The only thing about my humor was, sometimes it would hurt feelings. However, at that time, I could care less because I didn't want to be in Miami, although it is a city that I now love. I passed the class with an A-, because I was still slouching while speaking during my final speech exam. My days in Miami would soon end, because my mom lost her job and couldn't keep up with the rent or bills. She tried her hardest to be responsible for herself and me, but sometimes, even the strong have to take a loss before they can be victorious. I did want to move back to Boston, but if you have ever been to Miami, you know that the southern hospitality is indeed top notch. Southern hospitality is what many people need in life. It feels great waking up to pleasant weather and friendly people who want nothing in return for their friendliness. Miami provided that and more. My family in Miami is crazy but loveable. I was taught the meaning of respect, and the value of earning something I wanted; but with lessons of value also came lessons of hardships. Southern people support each other. However, as a teen, I was envious of my classmates for always having the best clothes, video games, and the money to play sports that weren't a part of a school. I didn't know the art of the grind while living there. I had never experienced living in the projects until I arrived in Dade County. I didn't know how to handle seeing my mother struggle and fight to provide for me, while she busted her ass working. I never really enjoyed myself in Miami, and it was my choice to return to where I was born and currently reside—Boston.

High School is always fun if you surround yourself with the right friends, and involve yourself in certain activities. My first year at

Hyde Park High School in Boston was an experience I will never forget. The odd thing about being back in Boston was that I missed my mother so much I wanted to return to Miami. I missed the sun, the atmosphere and my family. When I felt this way, I would remind myself why I wanted to be back in Boston in the first place. As usual, I played the shy guy role during my first two months in a new school until I was comfortable enough to make friends. I paid close attention to who I spent my time with and established relationships with. The three years I spent at HPHS, I never dated anyone from the school. I had a summer girlfriend, but she lived 45 minutes away, and my immaturity also killed that relationship. My mom soon joined me back in Boston a few months later, and that helped ease my mind.

I started playing basketball on the junior varsity team at my new school; because of my experience the year before in Miami, I felt like I needed to prove to myself that I could play the game that I loved. I attained my goal, by averaging 13 points and being appointed captain, by Coach Steve Wilson. He was a man who would soon become a good father figure and great friend. During the first week of practice, three guys made the basketball team; both Junior Varsity and Varsity. If you have ever been a part of Coach Wilson's basketball team, you would know that all of his favorites receive a nickname. I was given the name Miami, for the city I represented, but also disliked in a way. I became a favorite around the school as soon as the season started; our record was poor but I never had that much fun on and off the court. I think the way our peers cheered us on, even if we lost helped make it a great experience. Maybe it was the way people recognized and acknowledged us in the hallways. In any event, I didn't know how to handle this popularity, so my grades begin to slip.

Along with my Miami swagger and attitude came a heavy Southern accent that the girls seemed quite fond of, so I used it to my advantage, even though my English teacher was definitely trying to break my habit of stretching words and abusing the English language. I was more concerned with making girls smile and people laugh hysterically, than doing homework and studying. The next few years were a repetition of displaying my passion for playing sports, making my peers laugh and flirting with girls. In other words, I felt like I was "the man!" No one could tell me anything. In my opinion, I was great with words when getting out of trouble. The only exception was Mama Barthell; she saw right thru my bullshit 88.2% of the time. She's the only person who could bring me down from cloud nine, and would be the first person to tell me to stay humble and remember the times when I had nothing.

During senior year of high school, I realized my hoop dreams weren't going to come true, so I started being honest with myself. As a result, I joined the Drama Club. I was designated president of the club during the first week by a teacher who most students laughed at and disrespected. However, Mr.—let's just call him "Doug Funny"— showed me a side of myself that was always there. He taught me how to perfect my comedic timing, and balance it with a serious side while on stage. Before becoming a part of the drama club, the only acting I had ever done was lying to my mom or others to get away with shit. I co-wrote and starred in two plays during my tenure as president of the drama club.

Senior year was also I time that I began to become more active with the JROTC program, and discovered that I was a natural leader. This program also taught me how to follow, which is something I'm not used to doing. Becoming an effective listener was my main goal as a senior in JROTC, and I still use those tools today as an adult. I ranked fourth in my class with JROTC. I also represented our school during training and many networking assignments like "Boys State Massachusetts"; this assignment was set up to be ran like a small government type camp, and we voted on the President, Vice-President, etcetera. "Student State Trooper" camp was another aspect of this club in which I was able to show off the skills I had learned as a JROTC student. The club provided major networking for students, but I doubt if anyone remembers me from those trainings, although I attempted to leave some type of impression while being there. Most of the time, I was the only African American student attending from the city of Boston, so I wanted to make sure I didn't leave a bad impression to be judged on by the rest of the state.

Singing with my friends, was something I took up after basketball, and I also found a part time job to pay for prom and other things I wanted to do. I told myself I wasn't going to miss out on the things a student should never forget. However, before prom, graduation and college, I met a person who I fell in love with instantly, and I wasn't ashamed to show it. I promised I wouldn't mention any ex-girlfriend's names, so we'll call her "Ms. First." Technically, "Ms. First" was my first everything; from first love, first real sexual experience, and the first time I felt like I had to have someone in my life forever. I stated earlier that in Miami, I had my first sexual experience, but it was just oral; for years as an immature male, I would over exaggerate the experience. However, with "Ms. First," the experience was more meaningful. We were friends before becoming involved; she lived on the same street as I, and had a passion for basketball just as I did. Long story short, we were together for almost two years and watched each other grow and change drastically. My paternal family wasn't too fond of her, but they had no reason for their feelings. Their lack of friendliness toward her confused me, so whenever we spent quality time, it was either at her house, the house of a friend or another family member. She taught me how to depend on myself more, and showed me how to not give a fuck about anything anyone said to me.

During this relationship, I was very clingy and overly affectionate, which I still do. I would also want to fix everything, even if I couldn't and in retrospect, I can see how this would be a nuance, because I didn't care to think about how acting this way would affect my relationship. Unfortunately, she lost someone close to her while we were together; I didn't know how to handle that except to be there the best way that I could. I look back at it now and realize that some of the things I did were probably tough to deal with. Sometimes, I still do things that are not so great. I will still start an argument about the smallest thing, if my feelings are involved or if I am feeling attacked. Anyway, I initiated the end of the relationship, but in my defense, I felt as if I was forced to; towards the end, she did not seem happy. She also failed to be completely honest, and neglected me. Furthermore, I let people around us affect my decisions; I didn't know who to believe about certain things like infidelity and sexual preference on her behalf. I would soon learn she was into the same sex, which completely destroyed my mind and soul, because I don't know if this change happened right before the end of our relationship or after. Therefore, the demise of our relationship wasn't entirely my fault, and I still have a few questions that weren't answered during the break-up. My ego and pride was scarred, so I did what I could to keep myself busy by developing a new passion for music. I also hid the pain under drinking, which I'm no longer ashamed to admit. These two things replaced my love for basketball.

DAMAGED GOODS

In relationships, when you are aware that your current boyfriend or girlfriend has had a rocky past, I warn you to be careful. When you get involved with someone who has been hurt in a past relationship, this person is "damaged goods." Making a new relationship work will be a work in progress, and you will definitely have to be open-minded. This chapter explores the "damaged goods" and the "hero or heroine" side of things. In such a relationship, you have to work harder than in previous relationships. You have to be patient with the injured party, expect the unexpected, but also remember that you can't save someone who is not willing to be saved. Furthermore, people who have been hurt in the past believe that everyone will show their true colors in time. Therefore, once their future begins to remind them of their past, the other person in the relationship should prepare him or herself for conflict. You would be wise to remember that when things get rough in a relationship with someone who has been hurt, you cannot simply return the person to the state of mind they had before your relationship, as you would return an item to a store. People don't come with a receipt; what you see is what you get, so choose wisely. You have to be ready to fight, stick it out or leave.

Dear Mr. or Ms. Damaged Goods:

You have to realize your past is in the past, and you must let it go. You are with an entirely different person now. If they do things reminiscent of your past, it's okay to make them aware. However, avoid comparing them to someone who is no longer a part of your life. People make mistakes and people become accustomed to certain things; just as you expect your boyfriend or girlfriend to be a little more open-minded about your past situations, you must do the same. You chose to be in this relationship, and you have the right to leave at any time. If you do choose to leave, I must ask, "Why are you leaving in the first place?" This new person in your life gave you everything you wanted in a man or woman, so what's the problem? I hear people like you complain about good shit all the time: "I'm not used to this," "You're scaring me" or "I'm me, so don't try to change me." How are they trying to change you? How are they scaring you? Get used to experiencing good things in your life; you deserve it, silly. Especially when you're holding up your end of the bargain; but wait...are you?

You have to get rid of that baggage; it doesn't look good on you at all! Once you step into a new relationship, you must learn to do the following:

1. Realize everything isn't just about you anymore
2. Understand a new relationship means a new beginning
3. Learn to let go and move on.

If you decide to be a part of a new relationship, then let the past remain in the past. Although I do want you to learn from the past, to avoid making the same mistakes, I also want you to enjoy this new moment and this new experience. Being given a second chance to obtain security, commitment, and being in love is something that doesn't happen for everyone. Don't be afraid to be happy or be yourself. I know it's not easy, but you have no right to make your baggage the responsibility of the new person in your life. You may not be aware of it, but piling the baggage on someone else can be done in various ways, such as mixing your old personality with your new one, and being selfish. Furthermore, using the new relationship as a temporary replacement or moving at your own pace without being willing to meet your new significant other halfway is a sign that you haven't put the baggage away. You subconsciously know that this behavior is not fair to them, because if they were to reflect your behavior back onto you, you would pack your baggage and move on to someone else to continue the cycle. This just causes you to continue to run from love and happiness. Remember, you wanted this relationship; you prayed for a good man or woman, and you were patient until he or she came along. So why fuck it up with your bullshit? You are still the strong wonderful person your new man or woman wanted in his or her life; understand that they could be anywhere, but they are there with you. Appreciate that and don't chase them away. Communicate with them effectively about any problems you have, but don't expect them to not point out your flaws. After all, being honest is what being in a commitment is all about; not just that the fact that you are in a relationship. You are an adult who deserves the best, but if you are not willing to give the best, remain single. It's not only about you or just about him or her; it's about the both of you, and learning how to remain on the same page with each other. You cannot expect anyone to comply with your wishes if you cannot do the same. It could be something as small as spending more time with your girl or guy, or something more significant that expresses your love for each other. This isn't grade school anymore, and you don't have to deal with the assholes, bitches, etcetera, that you dealt with in the past. When your new partner is meeting your every want and need in a relationship, just do the same. Stop pushing good men and women away because you can't get over what has happened to you before. They did nothing except come along, try to give you something different, and attempt to provide you with what you were deprived of in past relationships. Having your guard up isn't exactly misguided, and you are not the problem in your relationships. However, you may contribute to hindering someone from reaching their full potential when dating you.. I was once in your position, so I know about forcing good people away; I also know the consequences of being afraid to be happy. You don't have to shelter yourself from commitment, intimacy or having all of those things you may desire from a romantic association. Having such desires is what a relationship is about, as well as having an open heart that you are willing to share.

If you don't care about any of that stuff then continue being alone; there is nothing wrong with living the single life, but don't drag anyone else down with your animosity towards commitment.

If moving slow is good for you, then make sure it's also good for the person you are involved with. Sacrifices and decisions have to be made in order for you not to be concerned about your past, current and future bullshit. Being damaged goods is a choice; it is also a way to stay in motion without living your life the way God intended. I pray that you remove this title from your life, and that you will be able to enjoy a true committed relationship. Removing the title requires more than just starting a new relationship, however. Initially, the removal requires breaking down the walls to the city around your heart. Then it demands that the both of you work hard, and communicate. To reiterate, remember to let go and just be happy. That storm of your past is over, and in order to be prepared to deal with more storms in your current relationship, letting go is essential.

A new relationship means new arguments, new compromises, and new conversations. It also means testing one another's ability to learn each other in the bedroom, and keeping the flame alive. These things are important to maintain a healthy relationship, which means they will need your energy and time. So confront your past; accept it, move forward, and never consider rewinding back to angry, bitter, miserable place. After all, who wants that? This is a new era, so take control of how your relationships will be!

Dear Superman and Superwoman,

You are everything that your man or woman wanted and needed in his or her life, so why are you still inadvertently fucking up? Remove that confused look from your face, and let's discuss this new person in your life. You are dealing with a person who has heard and seen so much, that they won't believe you unless you ease up a bit. They are already with you, and although they could be with anyone else in the world, they are with you. So relax! You cannot force them to be someone they are not. Why did you get into this relationship? (Go ahead and think-I'll wait.) I am going to assume you got into the relationship because you felt like this was the person you have been waiting for, and their personality matches your wants and needs. I know I'm right. I know dealing with them subconsciously blaming you for their past is annoying, but what are you going to do about it; run away from another person?

According to a survey I did during the Spring of 2010, at least 44.3% of 740 people in the city of Boston don't complete the sixth month stage of their relationships, because they fear repeating their past. On the other hand, 15% feel as if their significant other is pressuring them within the relationship, because they haven't experienced what the boyfriend or girlfriend has.

You may feel as if you have nothing to do with these statistics, but you do. You contribute to this percentage when you don't take your time in a relationship, force your feelings upon someone, and try to put them in a place which they have to evolve to naturally and solely. In other words, stop traveling in the same book, but on a different page. You are a rare breed, so stop fucking the situation up. With time and patience, you can earn everything you long for. In the meantime, continue being you and continue giving the one you are with what they were missing. However, prepare for a backlash if they aren't used to certain things, such as communication, security and respect. Most men and women don't know the meaning of the words, "I love you." Neither do they know how to accept them. Love is supposed to come naturally; it is very sacred, so don't force it. I know you are doing everything you are supposed to do on your part but stuffing it down his or her throat isn't attractive or reasonable. Doing this makes you an asshole and gives him or her an alibi to end your relationship. Analyze your relationship; figure out what works, and what makes him or her distant. An excellent relationship is based off being open-minded, and learning how to love another person. One of the hardest parts about staying committed may be all of the hard work you have to put in to push past their hang-ups regarding days gone by. I told Mr. and Ms. Damaged Goods that they need to help break the walls down to their own heart, but it takes a lot of energy on your part also. Although I addressed you as such, seriously, you are not a superhero, so stop trying to be. You are simply a good man or woman who can help but you cannot fix everything. Your job is to maintain yourself and give your new love something positive to motivate them to continue the relationship. However, remember that no force-feeding is allowed on this trail to commitment. I know it's frustrating and it's difficult, because you are not the one who is damaged; but I don't know too many people who weren't there once before, so keep that in mind. Are you willing to work hard at breaking their walls down at a pace that fits the both of you? Can you prevent yourself from becoming impatient with them? Ultimately, being in this relationship is your choice, meaning you have the right to leave at any time. However, if you do choose to depart, would you know the reason why? Would it be because you are not willing to work hard? If so, I have news for you; with every relationship hard work is inevitable and it is required for any relationship to be successful. Relationships are blessings in your life, and should be treated very seriously. You are what society needs. You care about more than just sex, a title and comfort. You are a real man or woman, so back off a little to avoid driving your new man or woman crazy with your impatience. It takes time and energy to build up to marriage, children, and security. There will be times that you will fuck up, so if you think things will be perfect, they won't. How you fuck up is what matters though. I see you look a little confused again, so let me show you a letter I wrote during the summer of 2009:

Dear Ms._____ (you, yes you, or maybe you):

   Okay, I know you have heard it all, and you have seen it all. You have been wined and dined, taken on cruises and long vacations. I know that when I attempt to make you believe I am sincere, you will question my motives. How do I know? Because I've done it to people my damn self. I can tell you that I will always be there, and never leave but that will be bullshit, because it's a promise I can't keep. I never make promises I can't keep, because I fuck up too. Since I'm not perfect, I will continue to mess up, but they will not be huge fuck-ups. Just little shit that might get on your nerves occasionally, like saying something that will piss you off. Additionally, I might not show up on time when you need me. I also may get dates mixed up, or snore and wake you up. While making love, I might come up short some nights; but hey, it will not be like that every night babes. I admit I'm slacking, because I have no car and I'm addicted to Facebook, Twitter, and my blackberry. I'm basically saying, even though all of those "fuck ups," there will be great moments. After all, who knows your favorite food to eat like I do? Who knows how to make you laugh? Who knows how to cheer you up when you're down? ME!

   I can promise fantasies all day, but I will fall short, because fantasies are for fairyland and CSI: Miami. I'm trying to give you your own reality show, called "Me Loving You" Seasons 1-until you give up on me! The theme song will be Michael Jackson's "Lady in My Life":

"There'll be no darkness tonight
Lady, our love will shine
(Lighting the light)
Just put your trust in my heart
And meet me in paradise
(Now is the time)
Girl, you're every wonder in this world to me
A treasure time won't steal away

So listen to my heart
Lay your body close to mine

Let me fill you with my dreams
I can make you feel all right
And, baby, through the years
Gonna love you more each day
So I promise you tonight
That you'll always be the lady in my life ".

I know that I have to trust you too. I'm willing to let you be the one who takes me away from all the bullshit—exes, bad dates, talking to phonies and lames. I am willing to be with you step-by-step, and through our first everything. Through the first date, first kiss, first movie, first shared sexual experience, first lovemaking...all the way through, to the first time I look you in your eyes and say, "I love you, and I believe in you."

I'm, not telling you to immediately say yes to everything, or to say you trust and believe in me right away. I am asking you to give me a chance to experience many endeavors with you that will be worth the wait. Baby, we all have to go through storms before we reach paradise. The only thing I can do is be me. If that's not enough for you, I will never try to hold you back, no matter how much it hurts. I can only move on and continue being me. You want to know my name? Well that's not important right now, so just call me Mr. Reality.

I keep it real with you at all times; not the "real" that will tell you everything that you want to hear, but the real that you have probably been searching for ever since you started dating. I'm a man who has evolved from a sex crazed, careless, selfish, ignorant bastard, to a gentleman who speaks the truth. A man who knows how it feels to be hurt; who is now unselfish, open minded, and understanding. I know what I want and I know what to do to not only get it, but keep it. Ms._____ (you, yes you, maybe you. Is that you?) You just have to be willing to accept happiness and to fill the void to overflowing.

As I mentioned before, I am sure you have heard and seen it all. You probably have had guys saying one thing, only to do another. Or maybe guys who did it all, such as whispering sweet nothings in your ear and stroking your ego with compliments and material things. You have probably even encountered another Mr. Reality, but drove him away with your past emotional baggage; but I have done these things too! Believe it or not, Ms._____ (you; yes you, maybe you. Is that you?), we are the same but different. I'm ready for a change; are you?

The question is do you want it? Of course, you don't need it, because you're in tune with yourself; you love sleeping alone, you enjoy being lied to, bullshitted on, and enjoy socializing in the same circles you have known of since you started dating. Sure you do...don't you?

A regular guy, probably from LNU, has told you he can get you tickets to his "magical kingdom" or that magic carpet ride; instead, you end up in "It's a Small World" while riding a winged throw rug. I can give you nothing but pure happiness and honesty, while those other guys give you bullshit and their manuscripts from Little Nigga University.

Sincerely,
Mr. Reality

That's just me, but you are different. You are special because you either withdrew from LNU, or never attended the school in the first place. Be patient, be adventurous and be prepared to make mistakes. You are just who someone needs in their life. Continue being yourself, because you are who a man or woman should crusade for.

MY LIFE (PART 2)

During the summer of 2003, I began hanging out with a group of friends from Hyde Park High, and we accidentally became a music group. Melvin Casseus had been my best friend since we met; I always joke that he forced me to become his friend because his cousin and I were great friends before he started following us around as an underclassman. Melvin called me unexpectedly one day during my freshman year at Bay State College, after I had become very distant from our friendship. Up until then, we would play video games all the time, and he would attend every basketball game to meet girls. When he called, he told me two other friends were at his house, and suggested I should come by and clown around like we used to. I knew Juan Harnett, who was one of the two friends he had invited over. Juan and I met in class my senior year of high school during a hyped up classic singing battle in the gymnasium after school one day. We still debate over who won that battle, but overall it was a great way to attract women and attention. However, I wasn't familiar with Luckner Alteon. I actually didn't believe that was his name for an entire month. The four of us didn't instantly click at first; my attitude can be very overbearing, and as mentioned earlier, I naturally lead and have a tendency to take over situations. Melvin has always had an I-don't-care attitude, which in my opinion, affects his judgment to this day. I'm sure that even as he reads this, he's either shaking his head or shrugging his shoulders. Luckner, known by everyone as Luk-E, was always the little brother of the group and still is. On the other hand, I bumped heads with Juan until we became roommates and got to know each other better. We went through many names during the time we were a group; the names ranged from Forte', Final Touch, to N'Trigue. Overall, we had fun and did things bachelors are known to do. We treated each other as brothers, and added another member to our group during the fall of 2005. His name was Jeff Jean Baptise; he eventually replaced me when Juan and I got into a heated argument the summer of 2005, which led to us not communicating for the remainder of the summer. This behavior became repetitive in our relationship as friends. Juan instantly felt a rapport with our chemistry of arguing and clowning around. We had tremendous rehearsals and ferocious debates over our personal choices in women, and life decisions. I won't get into each member's preference in women, but I will say I wish everyone the best in their relationships. Eventually, the group broke up because Juan felt that it was best for him and his family to move away from Massachusetts. Jeff was constantly late to rehearsals and became a cancer to the group; Luk-E made a drastic change in life. He went from being the little brother of the group, to trying to be a man too fast. However, he didn't want to take a man's responsibilities, Melvin maintained his I-don't-care attitude towards life, so he and I were the only two left standing. However, I also evolved.

I had two girlfriends during my singing days, and both were a major learning experience. I dated "Ms. One Second" for approximately four months, but at the end of those four months, I discovered she was six months pregnant. "Ms. Third" lost faith in me as soon as the singing group ended. So, in between and after each relationship, I lost control of my sexual appetite. I was a bachelor; I abused this title, did whatever I wanted, and always got what I wanted. I was the type of man who used the title "single" to my advantage, and didn't care who I hurt in the process. I also used my title as an entertainer and singer to get women to visit our apartment. (I won't detail the groups' adventures, as I am saving that for a follow up book, but in the follow-up book, I will expose all that went down during our studio sessions and parties. I refuse to leave anything out of that book, even if it affects anything. I feel as if it's the past, but you can't run from it. You accept it and move on with your life. You are responsible for your actions and if that book of untold stories reflects any lies, then that's not my intention, because I intend to be 110% honest. I will even reveal a few personal stories.)

When the group disbanded, I was only 22, and I was ready to party. Melvin and I partied hard nearly every weekend; we found ourselves becoming popular not only with club promoters, but with women. At that point, popularity and women was all that I cared about, along with my newfound passion for writing. I flirted my ass off, and I either told everyone I was writing a book, or I told them I was once a member of a singing group. Those were my pick-up lines with women. I never lied, but in retrospect, I realize I was a little deceiving because I didn't care about anyone's feelings but mine. I let my past reflect my future; I used the old excuse, "I've been hurt before" or "I'm not ready," knowing damn well I was full of shit. Most men do that; we use excuses to hoe around. However, some women were doing the same thing, during this time in my life, so that fit well with my agenda. For years after, I yearned for love. However, I felt like karma was kicking me in the ass because of how I had seduced women, and the way I presented myself as a clean-cut, no drama guy. Truth is, I was heartbroken by many ex-girlfriends and potential girlfriends. Eventually, I began to force myself to not fall for someone quickly, or I would purposefully be an asshole after we had sex. My only motivation for dating was sex, sex, sex, and more sex. I believed that if I had sex with many women, it would ease the pain. My motto was, "As long as you're honest, you can't get hurt." I was very wrong about that.

A few years passed, and I started writing this book. However, it wasn't inspirational or helpful at all. The very first edition of "Women R Stupid and Men R the Reason" was very angry and misleading. I thought I knew everything about the opposite sex, which led me to believe I had all the answers when it came to relationships. I remember talking to a woman who presented herself with such class and had the qualities that any man would want in a woman. I ruined the potential for a relationship because I became so excited, I fucked up and didn't even realize it; these unintentional screw-ups became a trend in my life. I would try so hard to make things work that I would come across as very unattractive and unbearable. I actually thought I could turn the bachelor switch on and off as I pleased. However, it's not that simple. The chapter, "To Be or Not to Be" explains why. After concluding that maybe I should just be single for a while, I started evolving again, I started to see life and how I lived mine differently.

Although I continued to be honest, there were still some situations where I did the wrong thing.

Another woman came along, and I thought she was different. I'll call her Ms. "Never Again." Ms. "Never Again" had a two-year-old son, who I fell for the first time I met him. In the past, I never dated anyone with a child, because I didn't want to deal with extra drama. However, she seemed different, although since we met on the social network Myspace, I should have known the relationship was doomed from the start. Since I was embracing my bachelorhood, my motives were to have sex and then tell her "seefuckyalata." However, things didn't happen that way, and I soon paid for it. After all, when you meet someone and have sex with them the same day you meet, you're setting yourself up for failure. We tried to pursue a relationship together anyway, and I knew telling family and friends that we starting dating after she commented on my Myspace pictures would not go over well. Therefore, I did what most would do; I came up with some realistic lies and bullshit, but eventually had to tell them about the craziness and regrets.

The first 3 weeks of our relationship were smooth; we had fun, sex and shared stories. I would take pictures of her and myself and post them all over my Myspace page. Some people, mostly women, were angry with me because I was always talking noise, although the relationship had just started. I thought she was the one, because she presented herself as the fun-loving, let's chill type of woman, who even encouraged me to play my video games.

Everything changed when I made the horrible mistake of moving her in with me and my two roommates, in Revere, Massachusetts. When this ungrateful woman didn't even thank me for doing her a favor, I should have known I was making a mistake. Furthermore, she was not even packed and ready to move when I arrived at her house, with a truck I supplied. However, she needed a place to stay, so as her man I provided.

The first week was horrible. One day, I had worked a nine-hour shift. Afterward, I played basketball with the fellas, only to come home to a dirty house and no food waiting-not even uncooked food, so that I could cook. I should have shown her my "Miami" side then and kicked her ass out. My mentality shifted that day, and I began to wonder, why the fuck did I allow her to stay there, if I couldn't even come home to a clean house or a prepared dinner. I received no explanation from the argument that followed, so I just sucked it up and fixed us a quick meal; I didn't think there was any sense in a child going hungry because of his mother's dumb actions. Things went downhill from there; we would get into arguments every single night regarding her whereabouts. While her child was with his father or grandmother, this woman would leave my house while I was working, return around one or two in the morning, and expect me not to say one word. Her behavior just caused more arguments and increased my suspicions. We also argued about how her son was raised under my roof. My mom taught me that if I wanted something from an older family member, I should show respect; if I didn't, there was no such thing as a "time-out"; she would simply give me a whooping. I'm the type of guy that expects upfront honesty and respect during a relationship.

The climax and ending of this nightmare began when she locked herself in the bathroom and cut herself, claiming that I drove her to it. At first, I almost took responsibility and apologized; days later I reneged my statement. This relationship started to affect my work ethic, and my writing abilities. It also started damaging my relationship with friends, which is something I usually never allow. Due to this drama, my friendships with my boys went through the ringer. I hated not being able to hang out with them or be myself. As time passed, my "spider senses" were at an all-time high; the more she said, the more pissed off I became. I don't like being lied to, and I can't stand when someone is hiding something from me. I eventually couldn't take it anymore; one night her mother called me inquiring on her whereabouts. I was embarrassed to admit that I had no idea where she was, although she was living with me. Therefore, the liquor started flowing, and the beer bottles began piling up; the whole time my anger raged and my mind played all different types of scenarios. The eye of storm passed, I finally grew concerned, and I hoped she was okay.

Later, a former friend of mine asked me, "Steven, do you know where your girlfriend is?" Of course I lied. I eventually found out the truth through photos; photos of her hugged up with and kissing another man. My "spider senses" then transformed into "LNU senses." I was torn and hurt, and immediately unleashed the angry Miami side in my blood by tossing all of her clothes in boxes and piling her belongings in a separate room. I confronted her as soon as she walked into the house. She was dead to me, and in my heart, she was just another woman. With tears and rage in my eyes, I heard myself yell, "Get the fuck out of my house and kill yourself!" I really didn't think she would once again lock herself in the bathroom and try to do it. The guilt fell upon my heart and for a split second, stupidity clouded my judgment. The guilt overrode my anger of being a man who had just been cheated on; naively, I let her stay at my house for a few more nights until she was able to move out. However, in the days leading up to her departure, I didn't want to be around her or even be in the same room with her.

One day, her phone received a text while she was in the shower, I read it, and didn't like what I saw. I sent a mass text to all of my female friends saying, "We have an official cheater in the building, and she needs to be knocked out." We argued about the sexual text message she received and I told her she had two hours to get her shit out of my house or the things would be thrown out. Of course, she began threatening to harm herself again; then "Miami" officially took over my body and I stated, "I don't give a fuck! You are fucking crazy, you bigoted bitch." She slapped me and I froze. An hour later, her mother called and asked me for enough time to get her things out of the house. I haven't seen that woman since, and have no plans to. I hope she reads this book and gains the message.

Afterwards, just like with any breakup, I chose alcohol as a temporary tool to get over it. I went out with my friends, and got so drunk I would be out of my mind. I got so drunk once, I threw up at least three times that night and twice the following morning. I thought I could drink my pains away, but of course God showed me that I had failed with that solution.

Strangely, about two months later, I began dating a woman who I once again thought I was going to spend the rest of my life with. I will call her Ms. "She's All That," as she was all that and more. We had been friends in the past, and we had a great chemistry. She was also a major fan of my web videos and blogs. Unpredictably, she was helping me get over my previous relationship, when we found out we had feelings for each other. I didn't think the relationship would flourish, because she was on the west coast in Las Vegas. So, although I didn't invest too much thought in it, it was fun to talk to someone over the phone who knew me, and who could make me smile and blush.

My 24th birthday was approaching and the popularity of my web videos and the content of my book was increasing. The concept for the book at the time was very controversial, and was similar to a do's and don'ts of dating manual. I was passionate about explaining how to be a man and how to be a woman, although I was failing to do as I said. I needed to celebrate big and I wanted to have as much fun as possible, so I contacted my favorite promoter at the time and gathered my crew of "clowns" to celebrate my awesomeness. Only eight of my friends showed up but that was okay, because I didn't care. I started drinking around 4:00 that afternoon. That evening would change my life and eventually my summer.

Melvin, late as always, picked me up from home around 10:30 p.m., after I'd told him to be there by 8:00. We drove to Club Rumor in downtown Boston and partied the night away. Ms. "She's All That" tried, but couldn't come celebrate my birthday; I wasn't mad at all, because I still didn't know how our relationship would turn out. At the club, I started drinking shots of 151 Bacardi Rum alcohol, then switched to tropical drinks. Eventually, before the night ended, I was downing anything in the cup without asking what it was. I felt like I just had to party and I needed to get drunk. (Please note that Melvin only had two drinks the entire night.) The last thing I remember after we left the club was going to McDonald's, and throwing up in the drive thru; everything after that was a blank. I woke up as I was being lifted into a paramedic vehicle, as cold rain fell on me. Melvin, who is known for falling asleep at the most random times and places, fell asleep behind the wheel; we crashed into a guardrail along the Revere Beach Parkway approximately 10 minutes from my house. I sustained fractured ribs, a sprained ankle, and a pair of lacerations along my head that will be there for the rest of my life. Being stuck in the ER for the remainder of the night had me scared for my life. I received the worse hospitality of my life at Mass General Hospital; I was still picking glass out of my head for two weeks after being released, and the treatment I received once the doctors cleared me didn't console me at all. Even with the horrible hospital treatment, I never thought I would be dissed by my brothers and friends. I had nearly lost my life with Melvin, and he abandoned me to find my own way home. Juan, his wife, and the mother of Melvin's child came to our aid while in the hospital, but afterward, I was left in the ER to find a ride home. I will never forget that, and the resentment I felt as a result would show, once Miss "She's All That" became a constant in my life. My two home girls Shayna and Maryanne, who I now consider sisters, came to my rescue in the ER; they made sure I had all of my prescriptions, and that I was comfortable in my home. Out of everyone who told me, "Steven, if you need anything, I'll provide it for you," the only ones who stood by their words were, Ms. "She's All That" and my mentor David Wright. Due to this, I cut everyone else off that summer because not only was I hurt, but I was evolving on my life journey once more.

I was lucky that night. I had no idea my life would change so much because of it.. Prior to the accident, I thought I was on top of the world. I had gotten rid of a problem, added a blessing and was living off the fruits of, as well as working for, the biggest non-profit organization in New England. The accident was a major wake up call for me, and my life in general. Miss "She's All That" arrived 48 hours after I came home from the accident and we clicked right from the start. We seemed to know each other better than we thought, and like a fool, I expressed my love way too early. However, to my surprise, she returned the sentiment, and I felt like she was the woman I was going to spend eternity with. I returned to work shortly thereafter. I found myself wanting to be around this woman every day, and began to discuss the future; I used my income to spoil her with cards, dinner, candy, and other gifts. If she had allowed me to, I would have showered her with anything she wanted. She was there to provide the affection and companionship I needed. I hung out less and less with the fellas, because I felt betrayed by the incident at the hospital. However, whenever they called on me, I tried to be there, but my heart wasn't in it and it just didn't feel the same. At the end of the summer, Miss "She's All That" and I began to discuss moving away from Boston. It was around this time that the small arguments began to turn into big heated arguments, along with mass confusion. This caused my guard to begin building back up, because it felt like déjà vu. My trust in her was starting to disappear, and so was my faith in our relationship. Nevertheless, I wanted to see where it would go, and didn't want to give up on her or our future. I started questioning whether her beauty, personality or my vulnerability after my accident had blinded me. Don't get me wrong; I meant every word I said to this woman, and I wanted to do everything I did for her. On the other hand, there were many unanswered questions. Why should I move in with this woman if she won't even let me meet her parents or be willing to meet mine? Why hasn't she discussed our moving arrangements with her sister? Why can't I completely trust her? Why ask this person to spend the rest of her life with me if I have so many questions? At that point, I knew the relationship would soon end.

I decided to keep grinding and working it out, in hopes that something would change. She wasn't a bad person, but the way our story ends seems as if I was played from the start. The plan was for her to move back to Vegas and get settled, while I searched for a job that would allow me to follow her. She moved at the beginning of September 2008. While she was in Vegas, I searched and found a few jobs and was willing to discuss my choices with her and my employer at the time. However, she decided she no longer wanted to start a life with me in Vegas, but thought Boston was the best place for us to be. I didn't mind either way; I just wanted to be with her, and let her know it didn't matter where we lived. I often felt weak in our relationship, because of my willingness to comply and agree with her every request; this changed very soon though.

In October of 2008, she contacted me a week after her birthday and broke up with me. I was shattered; even though I felt it coming, I had not planned on it happening over the phone, and especially not while in different states. During the time between her decision to move back to Boston and the breakup, I had begun to feel as if our relationship was getting stronger; after the breakup, all of those feel-good thoughts were erased. I asked her why she reconsidered, but received no explanation—only bitterness and anger. Her behavior left me totally confused and with no answers to assuage my confusion. However, she had no problem being honest about how she really felt. She used clichéd phrases such as, "I have love for you, but I'm not in love with you," or "our time has come and gone." This left me feeling full of rage. Afterward, I spent close to two months trying to come up with concrete evidence for why and how our relationship ended, yet I still have no answers. In a way, I felt played; I invested time, money and feelings into her, but in the end, I didn't get the same in return. My transformation upon experiencing these life lessons helped me to be sure and avoid anything that would cause me to relive similar situations I'd had with both Ms. "She's All That" and "Never Again." I became the ultimate bachelor for the next two years, with no plans to change my status.

Furthermore, my health took a major hit during this period; my body was finally fully recovering from the car accident, but my stress and eating habits caused me to be diagnosed with a peptic ulcer. This affects the stomach and creates a hole if not treated properly. A tumor developed off of the ulcer, and my doctors decided to remove it before it got worse. The doctors successfully removed the tumor, and I modified my eating habits from eating lots of spicy foods that I love so much, to indulging in little portions of those same foods (don't judge me). As I stated a few times within the chapter, I changed my personality, and with that change came new rules that every bachelor should live by. They are listed below:

1. Honesty is the best policy
2. You command women no matter what
3. Don't involve any feelings—it's either chilling or sex
4. Crew love is the only love
5. Be known for your career
6. Use the "seefuckyalata" motto; either take it or "seefuckyalata."

I lived by these rules for a while. I was very successful in obtaining everything I wanted from a woman, which of course, was SEX! I was so torn from the previous relationship with Ms. "She's All That," that I felt like I shouldn't waste anybody else's time or my energy on pursuing another relationship. I had given her all of the power in that failed relationship; since she took advantage of that, I became focused and was determined to make her pay for leaving me and the dreams I had for us.

The group I hung out with shrunk down to four; it included me, Melvin, Juan, and a high school buddy of mine, Leighton Lormeus. Our little entourage of brothers was the self-proclaimed best crew in the world. We always frequented clubs, having a great time and being ourselves.

(Remember, I have a book dedicated to every friend who spent significant time around me; writing about the crew will be a great follow up to my first book—okay, moving on.)

This bachelor attitude lasted maybe a year and half. Then, I grew weary of going on multiple dates, sleeping with women, and not feeling the emotions I wanted and deserved. I did meet some good women in the process, and they understood completely where I was coming from. There were also a few who didn't understand. I was being selfish with my feelings and really didn't care about their opinions, which was completely wrong, Sometimes I feel like karma will come back to me with high heels and a tight skirt.

I never lied or deceived a woman to get her into bed; I was brutally honest and blunt about the activities that would take place. However, telling the truth doesn't always make it right. Obviously, I didn't care about people who cared about me. Neither did I ever think about the consequences of having multiple sexual partners. I only cared about my feelings, my sexual needs and my temporary companionship.

I eventually eased up on my bachelor mentality and patiently waited for my queen to arrive.

I then began to pray to God to send me a woman who would not only fulfill every want and need that I desired, but also one that I would have all of the qualities for. I tried dating, but failed to find a woman with a good conversation who would allow me to see where things would go. This continuously happened, until I met the person I am currently with.

My written and video blogs were dedicated to finding my queen; I would focus on relationship issues that included bad dates, and the do's and don'ts of dating. I would invite friends as guests, and cut-up as a way to release tension via the web cam. My blogs were stress relievers, and were very popular amongst my peers and network. It became somewhat overwhelming to go into clubs and have random people come up to me and ask if I was the guy from the videos. I was popular in the city of Boston; some will acknowledge it, others will hate on it, which is another subject we will discuss later in the book. I had faith that my book and blogs were going to catapult me to marvelous things. I wanted it all. I wanted the fame, money, and most importantly, the respect. In September of 2009, I had my very first radio interview for this book and it went very well. I would like to thank 106.1 Touch FM for allowing me to broadcast my talents. Later that month, I held an event at a local club, for more exposure; it was also an opportunity to gain more fans and publicity for my name. I began building a name for myself, and would not let anyone hinder me. I held two more successful events within the year; the events were a stage to help promote local artists also. They performed with seven to eight minutes of material, and at the end I would talk about the book and have a great conversation with the audience.

In January of 2010, I had the chance to meet a wonderful woman by the name of Tiffany Starr; she wanted to interview me for her upcoming television show, *Shine*. This offer was very exciting to me, and was a great chance to demonstrate what I had to offer. After a few discussions, she offered to let me audition to become one of the show's hosts, and I jumped all over the opportunity. I was blessed with the job, along with the chance to befriend Lilli D and Regina, who are two other great hosts of the show.

Things began to look great for me overall. I had a steady income, great living arrangements, awesome friends, and my career was beginning to skyrocket. I had never felt happier in my life.

I was later introduced to Rochelle Levy, the publisher of this book, and we instantly hit it off. I made breakfast during our first meeting, and we talked for hours, like old college friends. After she outlined the logistics of what she could provide for my book and career, I made my decision on the spot. Once the decision was concrete, God started showing me who the real boss of the world is, and reminded me why I need to continue to give praise and honor to Him at all times.

I ended up losing yet another job, after being there for three years. With the loss of that steady income, went my apartment and a few friends. Once green disappears, some friends disappear also; it's bizarre, because I was never the richest man. I still struggled at times, with rent and bills, but I always managed to get by. Once I lost my job, naturally I had to decrease my clubbing and going out to eat. My spending habits weren't accustomed to not having money, and my bank account was not able to keep me afloat, after three months passed without a permanent job. Therefore, for the first time since my mom and I had spent the night in a hotel while living in Florida, I found myself homeless. I became very depressed and pessimistic about releasing my book, being on television, or ever getting married. Understandably, I was distressed about my lack of a home, and not knowing how I would eat on a regular basis. I take full responsibility for not being able to pay my rent or bills on time. I borrowed money I could not pay back, and lost between five and 12 pounds during my ordeal, since I was not sleeping or eating properly.

These life problems also affected my writing habits. Thankfully, I was permitted to re-vamp a few chapters that once focused on things I no longer believed, as well as introduce new chapters, such as including "Welcome to LNU." I failed to meet deadlines, but the publisher understood, reassured me that my book would be released, and explained that I should take my time.

This brings us to the present; the winter of 2010/2011. A few things have changed, though I'm still homeless and jobless. However, I work effortlessly on changing that status in my life. I have met a wonderful woman who has been nothing but supportive, and I pray she stays with me for a very long time. Of course, I finished my book, and my faith has grown stronger over time. The preceding was a short synopsis of my life; in my next book, I plan to go into detail about every secret involving my former singing group and crew. I have learned that the past is gone and nobody should get mad about the truth, from my point of view. Although history has proven that this will more than likely not be the case, I am prepared for the backlash and repercussions. Stay blessed, keep fighting and be strong. Now we return to the story within "Women R Stupid & Men R the Reason."

JOYS AND PAINS

Throughout the book I discussed how to overcome life situations, as well as how to not get caught in the trap of bitterness. How to avoid LNU was also part of the discussion. At this time, let's further discuss the joys and pains of relationships. Earlier in the book, I asked about your motives for being in a relationship. Have you figured that out yet? Courtship, love, learning and marrying has already been discussed; but are you afraid of love? Are you afraid of being hurt again? There is nothing wrong with being afraid; it is a common human emotion, especially when life experiences are the reason you feel that way. However, you can only continue to work at getting over your fears someday, because your fear or past does not deserve your energy, nor do they have the right to have that much control over your life. I also called you a champion earlier, and I'm sticking by my word. As a champion, it is time for you to fight any negative emotions. I know you are tired of being hurt; I know you are fed up with disappointments, and I know some of you have said, "I'm going to be single for the rest of my life." Some have experienced heartbreak, and some haven't; in my opinion, you should go through all relationship storms, so you can one day enjoy the paradise of the good ones. Without pain, there is no story, or room for improvement and growth. Even when you reach that "paradise" of a relationship, there will be problems, but not the ones that will leave you hurt or sad. I sometimes say, show me a perfect relationship and I will show you a perfect lie. You will always run into a few bumps in the road; despite all of the compromising you may do, no matter how great the sex is, or how many times you brush the little problems away. Taking the good with the bad is the ultimate sacrifice in a relationship. Living with the joys and pain you each bring, laughing through the good times and crying through the rough patches, toughens up a relationship.. I get frustrated when I hear about people seeking the "perfect" companion; yes, there will be people you are compatible with, and you will find a person who fits your wants and needs. Nevertheless, you will never find the "perfect" person to spend your life with. Perfect situations may be feasible, but the timing, mentality and motives of both people has to match. For example, you may find someone who doesn't want to get married or have children, at a time when you do. This does not make them a bad person, but it makes them incompatible to you, based on what you want and need. On the other hand, if you and the person are on the same page, that can make things a little easier for the relationship. That doesn't mean you have the perfect relationship. In my letter "Dear Ms._____(you, yes you, or maybe you)" from the chapter "Damaged Goods," I mentioned that in relationships, messing up is inevitable. However, it's not about when you stumble, but how you stumble. I have witnessed relationships breakup, because a person snores at night; I have also witnessed heartbreaks over miscommunication in the bedroom. We are so hard on each other, that some of us will never enjoy a healthy relationship, because we continue seeking a perfect one.

Let's start off with sex. Some of us definitely want a gentleman or lady in public and a porn star in the bedroom. We set these standards for each other, and if the person doesn't live up to the hype, we sometimes dump them instantly. We know what we want, but aren't willing to communicate or have the patience to teach our mate. This causes us to go in circles. That person may be a terrible lover in your eyes, but probably didn't have a complaint, until hooking up with you. The saying, "what may work for some, doesn't work for others," would be a perfect fit in this situation. However, most don't take that into consideration and label the girlfriend or boyfriend as a terrible lover. Communicate with them, put your ego to the side and have a detailed talk about sex. It is your mate's job to be willing to listen and learn your body. As a male, I know our egos are huge. We talk amongst ourselves as if we are holding it down in the bedroom, to boost morale and make it seem as if we are the best.

Furthermore, I agree with some when they say sex is very important in your relationship, if your relationship is sexual. We have the tendency to get so caught up in music and movies that we believe we are the perfect lover, and don't need to change a damn thing in the bedroom. However, this isn't how a relationship works; it's no longer just about you, and it is no longer about how you like it. It takes two people to make a great sexual experience, and one act of selfishness can ruin it. You may have hit it off automatically with a new partner; that would make things easier on the bedroom situation. Still, if they are not meeting your expectations, please communicate with him or her, in order to give them the choice to either fix it, or say "seefuckyalata." If this person isn't up to par in the bedroom, does that void the other things that attracted you to him or her? Do the jokes go away? Do the previous late night conversations become useless? Are you willing to just throw that away because he or she hasn't hit a home run yet sexually? With commitments, intimacy should be the key, and it takes patience and time. Although I think the physical aspect is important, try to get there mentally, and blow his or her mind away in that area first. Remember, this is the person who you decided to be with. You have the choice to leave at any time, but stick by your choice if you do decide to leave. Have a deep conversation with him or her and explain what you like and don't like when it comes to sex. Nothing is wrong with spicing things up and having a role-playing session where you are the professor teaching a new art; be creative. One thing you should not do is crush their spirits about not pleasing you. If you want to be pleased, then be willing to teach and teach well. The first sexual experience with new couples can be quite nerve wrecking and sometimes overwhelming. There are those who rush the process, and yet others are very slow to share their goods with each other. I am a huge fan of protecting what's yours, and not giving it away so easily. In the introduction, I mentioned that you should stop giving away your heart so easily. I'm going to say the same about your vagina and penis. There are too many sexually transmitted diseases out there that could have you scratching like "Willy Lump-Lump," so be careful. Another reason you would want to be careful is because some alumni from LNU have the mentality that once they receive the goods, it's time to seek out new ones. Protect yourself at all times and be choosy with who holds your goods. Enjoy your sexual moments with the knowledge that you will be pleased with a secure state of mind; resting in the knowledge that you will not end up contaminated after a few sessions of fun. What goes on in your bedroom should stay in your bedroom, except HIV, AIDS, Chlamydia, genital warts, Herpes, Gonorrhea, Hepatitis and Syphilis. They should never be allowed into the bedroom.

Don't be afraid of the joys of a great sexual experience; when you are sure that you are free to, have as much fun in the bedroom as possible. I suggest kidnapping each other, when feasible, and exploring your sexual limits. Once again, this applies only if your relationship has gotten to this point. Nothing is wrong with practicing abstinence or waiting until marriage, it's just not one of my personal choices. Here is a poem for a new couple experiencing each other for the very first time:

Tonight's The Night

Ironically, on this night there was a full moon, with its brilliant light shining into my bedroom window.
I have a feeling it's going to be a night to remember.
The dinner was perfect, the drinks were right, and I'm glad we decided to stay in, instead of going out tonight.
Without saying a word to each other, we knew tonight was going to be our night.

Passion is what we were after; we were seeking to take each other to the limit, because on our night we plan to play with each other's bodies as if they were musical instruments. On our night, we will transcend our mortal beings and break down the barriers that separate us from ourselves.
On this moonlit night, I plan on fulfilling your every little fantasy and arouse your inner most passion.
And I plan to speak no words.
I want to communicate through our touch and intuition.

We kiss; the first touch is a small one, the second one a keeper.
Our tongues meet.
An electric current too important to ignore jolts between us as we succumb to the magic of our kisses.
A flood of passion makes me pulsate with desire.
I then close my window as the heat outside dies and the night cold enters the bedroom.
Trembling, our naked bodies touch.
My flesh touches yours while yours touches mine.
I cover you the best way I can, as our arms tangle in the sheets; we grasp, we tussle, our thighs grip each other, and our hips thrust.
Oh shit, here it comes, as our breathing grows more intense, both of us vying for control.

You win round one and you climb on top laughing in the
moonlight.
While waiting to regain composure and energy, I think to myself
not only were you worth the wait, but I'm the luckiest man in the
world.

The night sky is a little darker and we begin again ten minutes
later.
As you place yourself into my hands, you give me a look telling me
to do whatever I please to your body; falling naked on the bed
opening up to whatever.
Our eyes meet as you submit to my gripping thrust; I feel your
fingertips grip my forearms.

As I pull your arms over your head,
You grasp the headboard, and for a second your body goes limp.
I blindfold you and watch as you anticipate for me to begin again.
You beg for my touch, but you feel only ice torturing, yet
caressing, your body.
I can see you clench the muscles inside your thighs, as the cube
teases the center of your bliss; the sensation is unbearable,
ecstatic you cry out, fantasizing the ice cube is a finger or tongue
and then your fantasy comes true.
As my nibbles trace up and down your torso, and I shower the
core of your body with tiny kisses and love bites,
You moan, wriggle, moan, wriggle, moan—is that your leg
shaking? I feel good about myself as my manhood makes your
body turn into molten liquid; your mind separates from your
body and goes someplace else; a place where everything is
sensation and all sensation is lust.

Your body is a furnace and I will be your fuel and fire.
Hearing our wet bodies slap together in unison creating perfect
harmony. We roll, we twist, we tumble in the sheets, and we
change positions over and over and over again.
As our feelings replace our thoughts and we give ourselves to
ecstasy, we work together in silence as we are both focused on
each other's pleasure.

Beads of sweat form on our bodies as we point ourselves in the direction of no return, with every pore and molecule yearning for release.
Together we are a machine, our hearts, bodies, and soul pumping as one.

Your eyes are closed as I try to end this thing on a good note; but damn, my hunger for you is insatiable and my thirst has no bounds.
Then your back arches, there is a straining cry for release and you collapse into my arms gasping for air.
Our passion is spent. We kiss, we let go and most importantly, we made love with each other for the very first time.
Because tonight was our night; on this night all things were possible and all things were real and extraordinary.
I believe we can now see the sun...yeah, that's the sun. You hungry?

Now that's passion and that was an ideal fantasy, something some people look forward to. This was a true story with a few fictional additions, but it is a fantasy adventure that some lovers want to reach. I'm no sex expert, but I do suggest that you don't take sex for granted, or take it lightly. If you are going to have sex, make sure you know what you are doing. Therefore, gentlemen, that means you should do whatever it takes to make sure she is satisfied and okay before you are. Ladies, it means, if your man is doing the right thing and isn't lying, cheating or any of the other things alumni from LNU do, you should do whatever it takes to make sure he is satisfied. The thing about sex is, some people are so selfish, they only think with their little heads and not the big ones. Some of us have even had that moment when we gave up the goods too early and woke up the next day in shock. When we make bad decisions, we have to take responsibility for that; we have to learn if sex isn't for us, and determine if we should wait until we can make better decisions. Blaming it on alcohol, emotions and anger are excuses; using those things is a sign that you are not ready for the power sex has. Here are some key points to let you know when you're not ready for sex:

1. If you can't fully unclothe, or don't want to be seen naked, you are not ready.

2. If you are not willing to do anything to please your partner, you are not ready.

3. If you can't stand the sight of looking at your partner, maybe you shouldn't be having sex, or maybe you need to find a brand new girlfriend or boyfriend. In any event, you are not ready.

This is very simple and easy to remember; if you perform oral sex, be prepared to protect yourself. STDs can also infect your mouth. Furthermore, practice how to perform oral sex correctly to avoid severely hurting someone.

Don't let peer pressure, music, pornography videos, the internet, television, or any other sources lead you down the wrong path. If you do not want to practice sexual activities, then don't. This especially applies to the junior high and high school kids who feel as if having sex makes them an adult. I'm speaking from personal experience— wait! Young men, I know that your raging hormones are going out of control, and you feel as if busting a nut is going to make you a man, but there is more to sex than putting your penis into some girls vagina. So, be careful!

Additional relationship pains include letting your friends and family get in between you and your girlfriend or boyfriend. When it comes to your relationships and your life, someone is always trying to tell you what to do and how to act. This includes me, but here is the slammer and the secret. Be who you want to be, and not who other people want you to be. I know my words and advice work, but if you feel otherwise, then don't follow it. It's your life, not mine; I'm just a guy who is trying to give you the tools to succeed in the real world. I want to help you think bigger and not settle for less. Seriously, how do you expect to get through life by being a follower? Even if you think you have all the answers, other people have the tendency to listen to their friends, family, and even pointless books or blogs that tell them how to conduct their everyday life. I know pep talks, similar to the ones I try to provide over my web videos, as well as this book, are helpful. In the end, it's your job to implement them. In relationships, someone is always there to put a bug in your ear to tell you how to react towards certain situations, or how to move forward or stay when you do not want to. You cannot let others influence you in a negative matter, or you will fail all the time. I especially have a problem with a woman telling a man how to be a man or a man telling a woman how to be a woman. You may be asking, "Steven, didn't you do this in the earlier chapters?" NO! I gave my opinion based on what I have seen. I told you that you really are beautiful kings and queens, who need to kick it up a notch and take care of your responsibilities. You may have noticed I was harder on men than I was on women. As a man, I know what we are capable of doing and how we can be better men. I can't show a woman how to be a woman; I can only give my opinion on what real men don't like, such as petty little girls who claim to be women. Ladies, if you felt like I was telling you how to be a woman, I apologize. I was simply giving my opinions on your faults. I see women as beautiful queens who are here to stand side by side with a man to make sure we all get to heaven.

I also feel that some people's expectations of a relationship is one where people live in a fantasy world, and want a happy ending with every single relationship they experience, instead of living happily ever after with the one they should be with. It sounds stupid, but it's a deep message. In other words stop fucking playing house! Your friends tell you that after a breakup you should date as many people as you can or in the words of my generation, "do you boo, or I'm doing me." Honestly, I can dig that, but doing you doesn't mean sleeping with your entire neighborhood, or the regulars in your local clubs. Neither does it mean finding the most convenient penis or vagina to screw, in order to get over heartbreak. Even if you were cheated on, sleeping around on the rebound is not good. This applies to both men and women; no double standards here. We put ourselves in these positions and lie to our own reflections, with things like, "I am good or I'm straight." Yet,, what are you willing to sacrifice to be great? What are you willing to sacrifice to have that dream relationship you ask for? Many people do absolutely nothing, but still feel entitled to happiness because of all the bullshit that they went through in the past. Reality shows us that this isn't the best way to go, because you'll find yourself going in circles and going nowhere in life.

Relationship advice is hilarious, because everyone has answers and is ready to tell others what to do, when their own relationship may be fucked up. We find ourselves listening to music for the answers on love, but to be honest there is no good love music out there anymore; it's all about sex, drugs and money. My generation is getting a bad quality of entertainment.

I grew up in a household where on Saturday mornings, my mother didn't care what you thought you had to do, and it was clean up time in her eyes. With cleaning came the sounds of, The O'Jays, Marvin Gaye, Jackie Wilson, Prince, Morris Day, The Time, Roberta Flack, The Isley Brothers, Bobby Blue Band, Cameo, Teena Marie, Rick James, etcetera... I mean she would dig deep into her collection, even to one of my personal favorites, Sam Cooke. That music had meaning. My generation thinks Bel Biv Devoe is old school, and doing the running man is the top classic dance. There was a time when you could hear the lyrics to certain music, and it would take you back to whatever situation you were going through at that time; we can rarely do that now. Therefore, there is no real point of turning to music in our day and age. It's just another temporary fix.

At the end of the day, it's all on you and how you feel. You can try to seek all the advice in the world and still end up with no answers. The people, lyrics or words from a movie or television script should not dictate the way you move forward with relationships or life. Those same people who dish out advice will be sleeping just fine, while you are still looking for answers to life's problems. It's great to ask for advice; it's also great to vent to a good ear. It's even better to read or do research on certain situations, but at the end of it all, who will be in the reflection once you look into a mirror? You! You hold the key to it all; it's your job to embrace this responsibility, and it is your duty to fix your own problems. If the problems are with your boyfriend or girlfriend, fix it with them. Stop turning to your favorite social networks like Twitter, Facebook, MySpace, etcetera, to vent or look for answers. Face your problems, and handle your situations without bringing in unnecessary people who are not really concerned about whether you are smiling, crying, happy or sad.

The joys of relationships come after accepting you will have issues. Enjoy the moments that are in front of you and take advantage of the situations. Know when to pick your fights within your relationship and remember to consider your significant other's feelings. One of the most satisfying feelings you can get in a relationship is a feeling of confidence you have in the person you are with, after you know you don't have to worry about infidelity or lies. After this is established, everything else falls into place.

Just as sex helps keep your relationship intact, teaching is sometimes required in order for someone to know how to love and be with you. Some adults shun this notion because they feel as if they should be accepted as they are; it is one's God given right, as a United States citizen, to do so. However, without sacrifice complete happiness is nearly impossible to attain. A commitment is a little deeper than all the clichés that are thrown around; it is also stronger than some people believe it is. A relationship is about communication; just talking isn't communication. You cannot be afraid to tell the person you are with everything! No secrets should be withheld, and no disrespect should be shown while you are communicating. Talk, don't attack, because attacking causes more problems. Attempting to communicate with an accusatory manner is the same as pointing fingers and withholding your true feelings. You also have to listen to your boyfriend or girlfriend, and pay attention to their words and body language. You have to keep in mind that this is a new person in your life, so you have to teach them. This doesn't mean you have to take them by the hand and baby them, but let them know what you expect from the relationship and what you don't like! This is one of the biggest parts of communication. Letting them just figure everything out on their own every time is very dangerous and will frustrate you. Relationships are all about give and take; you have to remember that everything is not about you. I continuously repeat and stress this point, because it's the key element. So, again I ask, what are you willing to do to get the relationship you want? Are you willing to teach them how to love you, while you learn to love them? After all, what's the point of getting into a relationship if you are not willing to fall in love? Why waste time just spending time together with no future plans?

If you are not willing to do anything to compromise, then why are you in the relationship in the first place? Do not waste anyone's time. You must know what you want, or risk the chance of hurting someone tremendously in the process. All the things I stated will not happen overnight, but should be worked on together. It's not about being all over someone or being completely passive. It's about balance; not only meeting them halfway, but walking with them side by side in order to figure out what the both of you need to do to make things work. Be honest with yourself and him and her at all times. Being in a relationship is a privilege and a choice! You can end it at any time but think before you do. Ask yourself, is the person honest? Do they treat you with respect? Are they communicating with you? Do they care? Why are you with them? I think a breakup should occur if a relationship lacks respect, fidelity, honesty, and doesn't fit your criteria for a long-term relationship. Remember you are a warrior, you are strong, and you are in control at all times.

The "Joys and Pains of Relationships" chapter and the "Courtship, Loving, Learning and Marrying" chapter go hand in hand. At the end of the day, you have to figure out your motives, your requirements and if you're willing to fight the good fight. You court, you learn, you love, you marry and you go through joys and pains.

ABOUT THE AUTHOR

Steven A. Barthell has been making a name for himself with his web show, "Stevens Thought of the Moment" brought to you by NbucketTV on YouTube. On the show, Steven gives samples of his debut book "Women R Stupid N Men R the Reason" and gives his thoughts on the activities going on throughout today's society. Periodically, he has guests from the local community, which include music artists, fashion designers, models, promoters and other positive figures in the Boston area.

He is also the host of Boston's newest show "Shine" shown on BNN Channel 23. While trying to put a positive stamp on this world, Steven enjoys keeping Boston on its toes with his quirky yet inspirational daily quotes.

Steven takes pride in growing from his past situations, and wanted to share his trials and tribulations in his debut book, "Women R Stupid N Men R the Reason." Steven resides in his birth city of Boston, Massachusetts, but isn't ashamed to tell everyone what city he represents; the good ole 305, Miami, Florida where he was raised.

Steven is an advocate for healthy relationships and bringing the old school mentality back into our society.

... AND NOW...

A sneak peek at the upcoming novel
by C. Porter:

SHADOW PRECINCT

For more information on workshops, services or upcoming releases;
visit: www.AzizaPublishing.com.

Prologue

A typical January evening in what was once New York City. The gate keeper, Lady Liberty, stood beckoning the masses to improve their wretched lives by becoming willing ingredients in the melting pot. The time when NYC was the world's city, a proverbial gateway for anyone from anywhere to pass through, frothing at the mouths for a taste of the American dream, is gone. Now, New York City is relegated to a part of the Metropolitan Corridor, the palm of a huge hand comprised of the largest cities in the Northeast sector of the United States. The individual identities of these collective cities reduced to fingers of the same hand, a sprawl of urban veins connecting the major organs of the Metro Corridor together. Dark clouds break apart to unveil the crescent moon's eerie glow, an almost unnatural iridescence radiating from it. The wind is biting, making the air prick like needles; a piercing, foreboding cold. Every now and again, the wind speeds up to sting your skin, whispering a polite "fuck you" as it rushes past your ears.

Standing atop an abandoned high rise building, overlooking a city that stretches far off into the horizon, he inhales deeply and lets out a sigh through the all black facemask that covers the lower half of his face. The long exhale from his sleek frame held so much weight that if any other person had been present with him, overlooking the skyline, they would have been able to interpret the unspoken words that dissipated in the recently expelled condensation cloud. Had the elongated sigh manifested itself into language it would have sounded something like; "fuck you, too"

The cold doesn't bother him. Fifteen years in zealot training will do that. The kids there are subjected to shit that the ordinary cops twice their age that patrol the basement population would have no clue about. He can hear the sirens now, a distant squealing like a dying pig. He chuckles to himself at the irony of such a thing. He imagined the cops down in base pop scrambling to get to the scene of the crime, scrambling to find validation as a legitimate arm of the law. But things are different now.

His father and his father's father were both in law enforcement but "Law Enforcement" has taken on a different connotation in itself these days. His grandfather, Francois Santeaux, was part of a dying breed of cops, police officers who had real, working, bullet-ejecting guns, and the right to use deadly force. They exercised that right often, for better or worse. He used to go by "Frank", as if to conceal the name that his French immigrant parents gave to him. Frank used to always say to his son Cyrus, "The whole world goin' to hell in a goddamned hurry". Prophetic words from Gramps, albeit his time table was a bit off. Frank was a cop in the early days of detective work, chasing tommy-gun toting bootleggers around, engaging in the types of shootouts that movies romanticizing the time period love to indulge in. Frank made a name for himself as a young officer in New York City during prohibition, pissing off Five Point bosses by routinely busting up their alcohol distribution operations and taking out low to mid-level goons with little regard for any type of protocol. There was a rumor that even the Chicago Police Department reached out to try to use Frank's services in the apprehension of Al Capone, to which he told them to go fuck themselves. Rumor has it that *that* was putting it mildly. His dad used to regurgitate the stories of his Grandfather's exploits. The amount of hyperbole increased as the years did. The crux was conveyed, however: police work is far less glamorous and more dangerous than any radio show, comic strip, or film. There's no second take when you're a stain on the ground. No stunt doubles.

Frank was a renegade. Being a white man that married a black woman in the mid 1930's solidified that fact. It was as if he had total disregard for the life a young mullato boy would face in an America which, as it turns out, was a bit more a la carte than the melting pot nickname would suggest. It rang of a narcissistic selfishness more than a love for his wife and the mother of his son. Reveling in the conquest of this amazingly beautiful brown skinned woman rather than having genuine affection for her. Frank's peers largely shared a restrained respect for him, his immense successes making them take their criticisms of him and his nigger wife behind closed doors as opposed to bringing these grievances to light in his presence. Luckily for them, they'd have an opportunity to let their choice opinions be heard faster than they realized. On the night of December 7th, 1941, the Japanese launched a covert attack on Pearl Harbor. They airdropped their Kamikaze soldiers over the base, where they dispersed and murdered hundreds of men, women, and children. On top of being ambushed, the Americans had no idea the ferocity that one exquisitely trained swordsman could display. When their katanas weren't enough, or if they were captured, they would ignite the bombs that they had strapped to themselves. They had no regard for their lives, which makes for a particularly dangerous opponent.

Frank turned up his old, barely functional radio to listen to Franklin D. Roosevelt address the American people:

"Last night, December 7, 1941—a date which will live in infamy—the United States of America was suddenly and deliberately attacked by Kamikaze swordsmen of the Empire of Japan."

Halfway through the speech he turned the radio off. He had already made up his mind that he would enlist in the Army. For all his self-hating, semi-racist ideas, he was a staunch patriot. Maybe because his parents found a place where they could prosper, but more likely because America afforded Frank the freedom to channel his urge to kill into a form of pseudo-justice, as praised as it was feared. A mere eight months later in August of 1942, Frank was deployed. He said goodbye to his wife with a long hug, but he didn't tell her he loved her. Deborah just made herself believe that he didn't say it because he knew he would be back. For years she had grown accustomed to Frank's callous nature, and she honestly believed that, deep down, he loved her dearly. He told his son he'd have a lot more stories to tell, this time he'd be, "getting his hands dirty with kraut blood". A then four year old Cyrus hung onto every word his father said. Like any son, he aspired to be just like the elder Santeaux; though he was too young to understand the type of man his father was, oblivious to the various bruises that blended into his mother's skin. Cyrus aspired to be that strong, even if the strength that he saw emanating from his father was a mutated perversion of it.

Frank left behind his black wife and his mixed son. God only knows how they would have fared in facing the more intense racism found in the Swamp Corridor, though it wasn't called yet. Frank and his wife did keep in contact via letters. She found it odd how affectionate he was through text compared with his demeanor in the flesh. If she had known the atrocities that Frank was witnessing on a daily basis, it would have been clear how it made him re-evaluate what was important in his life. Deborah would write about how much Cyrus was growing, how he asked his father to write stories of what war was like, and how they had begun attending a new church called the Disciples of Van Sant. She wrote of wanting to enroll Cyrus in a newly opened dojo and she raved about Eldrick Van Sant's anti-gun, anti-war message, much to Frank's chagrin. Frank was a man who knew very few skills that did not involve inflicting pain of some sort. In one of his letters, dated October, 14th 1943, he wrote: "No way will my boy be wasting his time with the karate. Why would I willingly choose to use my hands when I can just shoot you? Just because the world has been doing it, doesn't mean Americans have to bend. We're fucking Americans, that's the reason I'm over here to show these kraut bastards what it means to be one". Ironically, this letter was written five days after Frank witnessed a captured Nazi soldier beat 7 men, 3 armed, to death before being shot. The handwriting itself resembled a child's because he was scrawling with his left hand, his right arm had been broken in an encounter with a German soldier well versed in Nazi style Hapkido. He was saved only when an allied sniper clipped the German's leg, allowing Frank to plunge his combat knife four solid inches into the enemy's heart. That event had scared Frank shitless. He never let it show, though.

As the war was winding down, the situation on the home front was becoming increasingly tumultuous. While men like Francois Santeaux were deployed overseas, crime spiked as criminals jumped at the chance to fill the voids left behind. The Prohibition battle was still going strong, with Elliot Ness and the Alcohol Tax Unit doing their best to stave off the flood of violence. For his part, Mr. Ness and the Untouchables were doing an admirable job, but even they couldn't be in two (or three, or four...) places at once. Murder rates were drastically rising every year. The mafia and the various gangs in New York City were getting more brazen in their acts of violence. Children of district attorneys were kidnapped and murdered in the most despicable fashions, wives of adversaries raped and buried alive. It was almost as if the massive body count of World War II served as goal to try to surpass for the criminal population, a macabre carnival game that they couldn't win, but they would try. In December of 1944, newly elected New York Senator Robert Wagner was murdered on his way back to his home, presumably a mafia hit. On the west coast, the situation was no better. After the boss Joseph Ardizone of the Los Angles Crime Family was killed, a struggle between different factions veiled the city in chaos and violence. Eventually, Jack Dragna (born Ignacio Dragna) would emerge as the new boss of the LA Crime Family. When an unfortunate soul thought it would be a good idea to go to the feds with potential dirt about the new boss, he would wake up to discover the middle school that his children attended had been sprayed with bullets in the middle of the day. In a cruel twist of fate, this man's children survived the massacre. Thirty seven other children, most under the age of fifteen, were not so fortunate. This event sparked public outrage across the country and became another talking point for the charismatic Reverend Van Sant, whose following was growing as fast, if not faster, than the murder rate. Eldrick Van Sant would speak on these issues in what is arguably his most famous radio sermon, entitled "Lament for the Voiceless Fallen" on New Year's Day, 1945.

"The war is coming to an end. The time for investing in tools of death and destruction is over. We need to re-invest ourselves in the betterment of each other, our country, and Almighty God's green Earth. The Almighty Jesus Christ will smile upon us and America will be returned to a beacon of light that the world will look to in moments of darkness". ~Rev. E.Van Sant

It would be during this sermon, heard by millions across the country, that he would call for new legislation to restrict the use of firearms. Even if you were a gun-loving all-American, it's hard to debate your position when the opposition is claiming that Jesus is speaking through him. This growing public scrutiny was putting an increasing amount of pressure on President Roosevelt. He was in the process of trying to bring an end to World War II, yet the ever growing problems on the home front were requiring more of his time to address. FDR spent the early parts of 1945 deciding what his course of action should be in resolving these issues. By this time, not only was a large portion of the voting population enthralled with the fiery rhetoric of Reverend Van Sant, but the good reverend's constituency also consisted of lawmakers, congressmen, and United States senators. President Roosevelt reflected on these issues privately, recalling the failed assassination attempt in 1941 that left him paralyzed from the waist down; the shooter a radical follower of Van Sant's (Van Sant himself condemned the attempt citing the use of a firearm, which he was strictly against).

In mid-February, 1945, President Roosevelt, along with trusted members of Congress and the Senate, began to draft what he believed was the ultimate solution. Looking back upon his decision, it seemed as if he was taking responsibility for the millions of lives lost in World War II and in the war at home, his mind in a self-made prison of guilt coupled with a need to repent for his perceived sins in the face of his own mortality. I suppose all the religious talk was rubbing off on everyone in one way or another. The results of these private meetings would be the introduction of the 22nd Amendment which stated:

AMENDMENT XXII (1945) – ONLY DESIGNATED MEMBERS OF THE UNITED STATES MILITARY HAVE THE EXPLICIT RIGHT TO KEEP AND BEAR ARMS. A WELL REGULATED MILITIA, BEING NECESSARY TO THE SECURITY OF A FREE STATE, MUST BE REGISTERED WITH THE UNITED STATES MILITARY, PLACING THEM UNDER THE JURSIDICTION OF THE UNITED STATES MILITARY, IN ORDER TO BE RECOGNIZED AND THUS ENSURING THAT THEIR RIGHT TO BEAR ARMS IS NOT INFRINGED. FAILURE TO DO SO WILL RESULT IN SAID MILITIA BEING BRANDED A "TERRORIST ORGANIZATION", SUBJECTING THEM TO THE SAME RULES APPLIED TO ALL UNITED STATES CITIZENS.

This was in conjunction with the Arms Recollection Act:

CITIZENS WITH REGISTERED FIREARMS WILL BE CONTACTED FOR ARMS DECOMMISSION. FAILURE TO COMPLY BY TURNING IN ALL ARMS AND REGISTRATION PAPERWORK TO THEIR NEAREST POLICE STATION WITHIN 60 DAYS WILL RESULT IN A $2,500 FINE (SUBJECT TO INFLATION) AND 5 YEARS IN JAIL. AFTER 90 DAYS, THE PERSON'S NAME WILL BE SUBMITTED TO THE ARMS RECOLLECTION UNIT FOR FORCEFUL DECOMMISSION.

With one weak-handed stroke of the pen, President Roosevelt set into motion the single greatest change the United States

Constitution had ever undergone. On April 12th, 1945, he died, believing that he made the best decision to ensure that more lives would be saved for future generations to come. In all actuality, it was a grand introduction of shit and fan.

Frank, scarred in every sense from the atrocities that he had seen and committed, returned home in the summer of 1945 to a country that was experiencing its own identity crisis. The amount of Americans killed at home was beginning to mirror the amount of Americans killed abroad. The American public was still shaken from President Roosevelt's death, which added a bittersweet taste to the news that the final terms of surrender had been signed aboard the USS Missouri, effectively ending World War II. While a fair share of the American populace was rather outspoken in condemning FDR as a "war monger", a perpetuator of death, even if justified against a certified mad man such as Hitler, they were still hurt by the loss. After all, FDR had already served three full terms, which was an indication that, for all of their picket signs and tough rhetoric, many people still felt him fit to lead the country for all these years. Frank's own experiences were a microcosm of that. He was about as approachable as a fox infested with rabies, but that didn't stop the younger soldiers ("pansies" as he referred to them) from cowering behind him in the foxholes that peppered the European landscape, in hopes he would shield them from death. Sometimes Frank was successful doing just that, other times he was not. One thing was for certain; as time went on witnessing death affected him less and less.

Frank had found that the country he called home, much like himself, was full of contradictions. At times he felt as if he had come back to an alternate reality where things just seemed slightly off from what he remembered, bizarro America. He displayed a bit more affection to his wife, Deborah. She noticed the smallest increase in love like a fish noticing the slightest change in the currents of the ocean, and she was happy with the improvement, however miniscule. Frank's son Cyrus was seven years old when his father returned from war. Cyrus immediately noticed the physical change in his father, his right arm unable to extend fully due to the savage beating he took at the hands of a skilled Nazi fighter, his eyes appearing more sunken in and saddled with the bags that only sleep deprivation during wartime can bring. Frank's once muscular frame was now gaunt, his countenance appearing to age at twice the rate of every other part of him. Young Cyrus disregarded all of the blatant signs that pointed to the fact that his father was no longer the same man. The Purple Heart that Frank was awarded sat in the living room on an unsuspecting bookshelf, under a gray veil of dust. Cyrus would stare at the medal to the point that it was engraved in his brain. He could close his eyes and vividly see the indigo ribbon, the engraving of George Washington. He would imagine his father, Frank, in various wartime situations, getting his hands dirty with kraut blood, fighting the most skilled Nazi fighters. Cyrus had to rely on his own vivid imagination because Frank rarely wanted to speak about the war. He probably didn't want to appear weak in telling the truth about the paralyzing fear that he felt on numerous occasions or of his narrow encounter with death, an encounter he survived not by any display of his own ability, but by a sniper bullet fired by a nameless, faceless ally. He couldn't bring himself to lie to Cyrus or paint a portrait of himself that wasn't entirely accurate. One of the first instances of keeping it real ever documented. So he opted for silence or a sharp response, usually something to the effect of: "The war is over. You may not be able to read a paper but I'm sure you're not too stupid to understand the words comin' from the radio". Frank's increased affection to his wife was matched by an increased disdain for his son. It was his way of subtly trying to push his only son from following in his footsteps. He wanted him to avoid seeing the same horrors that he had. He didn't want his son to grow up believing that strength alone would be enough to make it through this life. However, by that time it was too late. Like his father after hearing Roosevelt's famous speech about the covert attack on Pearl Harbor, young Cyrus Santeaux had already made up his mind.

1956

Shortly after Cyrus graduated from High School, he notified his parents of his intention to join up with the Arms Recollection Unit, an idea that made his father unleash every curse word upon him that he had in his repertoire (which was quite massive). A recruiter had spoken to him about it, and, at least in Cyrus' mind, that was the perfect place for him to pursue his future. He had always wanted to be a cop like his father, with the rise of the ARU, he saw the opportunity to be more than that. Cyrus still held the naïve vision of that young boy who idolized his father, his green eyes lighting up whenever he spoke about potentially being a part of the ARU. He wanted desperately to show Francois ("Frank" had reverted back to his given name when his physical body began to match the weakness that he believed that name implied) that he would make him proud, that he would have his own accolades lined up next to his father's Purple Heart, which had stayed in the same place since Cyrus was a boy. In 1956, an 18 year old Cyrus stood on the stoop of his family's modest house saying his goodbyes to his mother and father. Cyrus was well aware that it'd be two years before he saw them again, since the ARU training was a bit more intense than the Special Forces training in the US military. Cyrus was excited almost to the point that it overwhelmed the sadness he felt from leaving the only family he had known. His heart was beating fast at the thought of being trained to be a weapon. The recruiter even let slip that the ARU had acquired the services of several martial arts masters from around the world to fine tune the new recruit's close quarter combat skills. He got goose bumps at the idea of killing his first man.

Cyrus' mother hugged him for what seemed like forever, he was eager to board the train that was headed to the nation's capital to begin his training. She held him close, and wept on his chest. He almost had to pry her interlocked arms from around his body. Her common refrain was to say how much she loved him and how she only wanted for her baby boy to return to her in one piece. Her words were shaky like a tight rope walker with the emotion that she felt deep inside, the same fear and anxiety she felt when the other man she loved went away to WWII. Most of her words went unheard by Cyrus, who was fantasizing about his ARU training as if it were a woman. The only time he snapped out of his trance like state is when he looked at his father, Francois, who said no words but was also in tears. Cyrus had never seen his father cry, he barely remembers ever seeing his father sad. Francois' sadness was most times reflected outward as anger. But here was a genuine sadness and the tears, though Cyrus could count them on one hand, said more than any words his father could muster.

The train ride seemed like it was an eternity. Cyrus was quiet; reflecting on what awaited him when he arrived in D.C. The instructions from his recruiter were cryptic; when he arrived in D.C., he was to go to Union Station. Once there, he was to just wait. They would find him and bring him to what would be his home for the next two years. The mysterious protocol added to the excitement of it all. He arrived at Union Station in the afternoon, he walked in, pea soup green duffle bag slung over his broad shoulders, and found a bar. He plopped his duffle bag down and propped his lanky frame up on a bar stool with a grin plastered on his face that he couldn't restrain. The bartender, busy wiping down the counter, looked up and made eye contact with this tall, beige-colored man, and for a moment the intimidation that he felt made his heart palpitate a bit faster. Like father like son.

"What can I get for ya?"

"Just a water, please."

"I'll take a rum and coke."

Both Cyrus and the bartender's eyes darted to where the gravelly voice was coming from. Their eyes fell upon a young, white man. The bright red hair atop his head was combed back in an attempt to seem less unkempt than he appeared. The stubble on his face was an indication that he had not shaved in days.

"Looks like we're headed to the same place...wherever the fuck that is."

Cyrus grinned, but his time it was a bit less sincere.

"Are we? You're waiting for the ARU pickup too?"

Before he answered Cyrus' inquiries he threw back the entire glass of rum and coke as if it was a shot. It seemed like it had an instant effect, as the inflections in his voice began to randomly spike in typical I'm-drunk-as-shit fashion.

"M' name's Gerald. Gerald Everett. Friends call me Jerry."

"Nice to meet you Jerry."

"That's Gerald to you. Lemme get another rum and coke."

Cyrus made nothing of Gerald's curtness. Deep down, he felt that he could beat him to within an inch of his life if he needed or wanted to.

Before taking a large swig of his second rum and coke, Jerry muttered in the general direction of Cyrus, "I hear a lot of people don't make it outta ARU training."

"Well, I don't plan on being one of those people...Gerald."

Cyrus put extra emphasis on Mr. Everett's government name. Jerry felt it, and he couldn't hide a smirk of his own at the sharp response that was just volleyed back to him. After about 15 minutes of sitting in silence, Jerry reveling in the effects of his inebriation, Cyrus laughing to himself at the thought of this dirty, drunk, dickhead inevitably failing out of ARU training, Cyrus' head jerked around at a shadowy image that invaded his peripheral vision. He caught a man, dressed in a black suit as if he was going to a funeral, approaching them with swift steps. The man's voice was deep, with the hint of a southern accent.

Cyrus Santeaux? Gerald Everett? Come with me please.

They followed the man closely, in silence. Cyrus' heart was racing, his mind in a state of shock that he was on the precipice of what he wanted his entire life. Jerry, every now and then, would mumble something unintelligible under his breath, the brisk pace of the man dressed in black's strides undoubtedly killing his buzz. They walked outside where another man, dressed exactly the same as the first, was behind the wheel of an all-black Chevy Belair. For an instant, Cyrus was reminded of the taxi's back home. That was the last thought that he would have of his home or his family for a long time. Jerry and Cyrus tossed their bags in the trunk of the Chevy with respective thuds. The man dressed in black opened the doors for both men and then sunk into the front seat. He didn't say a word to them as the quartet pulled off, didn't even spare them so much as a glance. It was almost as if they weren't there. Cyrus imagined this to be a subtle introduction into what life in the ARU would be like; the sacrifice of one's identity, the use of anonymity as a weapon. In all actuality, the man, who still hadn't introduced himself or the driver, didn't care to know either one of them. He had picked up many recruits. Most of said recruits didn't even make it out of training, the ones that did were going into a hellish warzone that they could never prepare themselves for. He failed to see the relevance of the formalities. One hour turned to two, two hours to three and all signs of an urban environment gradually faded to trees lining either side of the highway. By this time it was dark. Cyrus checked his wristwatch to see that it was approaching nine o'clock. Jerry had been sleeping the entire way, still subconsciously mumbling. A rocky jolt made the shocks on the Chevy squeak like mice being stepped on. It caused Cyrus to swiftly look up from his watch and Jerry to hit his head on the window, forcing him up from his alcohol induced mini-coma. They both looked out the window to see that they were now on a dirt road, going deeper into a forested area. Both men grew nervous, their heads swung around simultaneously to meet each other's gaze. In that brief moment that their eyes touched, all animosity that they felt for each other dissolved in an instant, replaced by a mutual nervousness that was exacerbated every time they looked out the window and realized they had no clue where the fuck they were. The Chevy slowed gradually to a stop.

"Get out."

Both the young men obliged the man riding shotgun, they walked around to the trunk and got their bags out. By this time the man was standing outside of the car, he continued to speak.

"You will wait here. They will be up shortly."

"What do you mean, 'up'?" Cyrus inquired to the man's back as he was slinking back into the all black Belair, as if he was going to receive an answer. The two men watched the car do a three point u-turn and leave out the same way it came, reusing the tracks that were dug into the muddy ground upon the convoy's arrival.

"What the hell is goin on, man..." Jerry wondered aloud.

The sounds of the forest were growing more intense and it seemed the heat was growing along with the noise. The two men sat quietly, still baffled at the predicament that they found themselves in.

"I knew I shoulda asked that motherfucker for his name...How do we know they weren't murderers and this isn't part of...part of their sick game? We could be getting hunted right now, and I mean right now, like we're deer man. And we're just goin' along with the goddamn program..."

Jerry had gotten himself so worked up he was pacing in the small circular clearing that they were dropped off in. Cyrus let him ramble on. He, too, was feeling a bit uneasy about the current circumstances. Jerry continued to pace and fire off profanity laced conjectures about what was going to happen to them if they stayed before he was cut off by Cyrus.

"Did you hear that?"

Faint grinding could be heard, but the direction of the noise couldn't be pinpointed. They both looked around in all directions as the noise grew louder. There was a look of coinciding shock, as if they had both witnessed the same crime and made a silent pact to keep it a secret. The sound was coming from beneath their feet. No sooner could they process this fact was it followed by the ground beneath their feet shaking ever so slightly. Both men picked up their bags and backed slowly from the area that they had occupied. Jerry leaned over and whispered

"We need to just run, bro. I think we can get away."

Their eyes fixated on a small rectangular light that was starting to peak through the dirt and forest debris on the ground. With another thrust, an elevator began to emerge from the ground of the forest. Both men were utterly speechless at the sight. The door parted open and a man, dressed in military attire with the credentials of a general adorning his uniform stepped out.

"Gentlemen, welcome to the Arms Recollection Unit. Please come with me."

1997

As the sirens faded off in the distance, he awaited the inevitable incoming message that was sure to follow. He stood at the edge of the building, mentally plotting his descent down to the trenches of base pop. He fondled the hilt of his katana, which protruded about six inches over his right shoulder. The blade itself was exquisitely crafted, a gift given to him by his fiancé. It lacked the typical curvature found in most katanas, even the shitty standard issue ones that new zealots received upon crossing. It was also longer than usual, 27 inches in length to be exact. It was carried in a shiny onyx sheath that was straight to match the shape of the blade. He rubbed his hand on the engraved lettering on the hilt:

Jusq'au mort faire nous part

As he predicted, his earpiece began to buzz with the slight vibration that indicated an incoming transmission. He had adjusted his comm. settings so that Warning by Biggie played when he got a call.

Who the fuck is this?
pagin me at 5:46 in the mornin crack a dawnin
now I'm yawnin, wipe the cold out my eye
see who's this pagin me and why...

He opened the channel by touching the accept button of the device, located behind his ear.

"Myth, come in…Myth, do you copy? Premier Myth? Do you read me??"

"Yeah, I'm here."

"The commish says he's found something that we need to check out."

"Does he now? That's a first, son. That prick acts so high and mighty until he needs us."

"10-4 on that sir. How do we proceed?"

Myth looked down at a small screen on his forearm; it lit up and showed a miniature overhead map of the city with four red blips, "I'm the closest one according to the location map. I'll rendezvous with the Commissioner, it's probably something mafia related…clean up more of their messes."

The voice on the opposite end of the communicator chuckled lightly, "Roger that. Raspy out."

He ended the transmission with the same motion he began it with. He drew another deep breath and re-traced the vertical descent he would take in his mind. With two large steps he leapt off the building with the grace of an Olympic diver, twisting in the air and dropping down towards the concrete, he dropped down two stories before reaching out to grab the iron rung of a fire escape. He swung off of it, the momentum propelling him through the air like a circus act shot out of a cannon. He rolled through the air and unfurled his body, he kicked off of the closest wall sending him in the opposite direction like a ricocheting bullet, rolling over a dumpster and landing on his feet in stride, running through the dark alleys.

People caught glimpses of something moving through the shadows, but quickly dismissed it as a figment of their imagination. Sons of the Shadow; zealots indeed lived up to that nickname.

The commissioner ducked under the yellow crime scene tape that indicated to the onlookers that something serious was contained within its borders. Most of them were more interested in seeing a zealot in person than the gruesome murder scene, something they could tell their friends at the next upscale dinner party.

"I actually *saw* one."

The commissioner pushed past the plain clothes cops and CSI investigators to see for himself the body of First Family boss Xavier Elizondo, arguably the most powerful mob boss in the Metropolitan Corridor, or any corridor for that matter. He hadn't been seen in years, delegating the day-to-day operations to his many underbosses. As the commissioner was about to open the already ajar bedroom door to view the scene of the crime, a young officer burst through the door, almost hitting him, vomiting in his hands. He glanced at the young officer.

"Clean that shit up, you might be contaminating evidence."

The commissioner pushed through the door. He was greeted by the smiling face of a young woman that he guessed was Puerto Rican. Her head was nearly split in half horizontally from the strike of a sharp blade whose impact was inside of her mouth, between her two sets of teeth. The blow created a grotesque incision that left her lower jaw hanging so that her chin was resting upon her throat. The amount of blood was surreal, some of it still moist on the silk sheets of the king size bed. Her eyes were open, indicating that she was alive to witness her own execution. The flashbulbs from the camera shots of the CSI investigators snapped the commissioner out of his trance. He followed a trail of blood to the large bathroom. He walked in and saw X, hanging from a rope that was tied around the toilet for support, and thrown over the rod that held the shower curtain. Elizondo was there hanging by his feet with his head face down in the bathtub with both of his wrists slit as well as his throat. He was missing three fingers from his left hand.

"Ho-leeee shit."

After standing in the bathroom, looking at the portly, lifeless body of one of the most powerful leaders of organized crime in the country, he stepped back into the bedroom and beckoned for the lead CSI investigator so that he could pick his brain for a bit.

"Dunbar."

"Commissioner Archibald."

"What ya' got for me?"

Dunbar paused for a moment, "We got the call about 4 hours ago, some of the neighbors heard a loud scream, we assume to be the first victim you see over there."

"Any idea on who the ventriloquist dummy is?"

Dunbar's eyes shot away for a brief moment, seemingly taken aback by the crass reference to the gruesomely murdered woman who laid no more than ten feet away from them.

"No ID on her, probably gonna have to run a finger print scan. My guess is that it's probably a call girl."

"Man, talk about picking the wrong dick to suck, eh?"

Commissioner Archibald paused to light a cigarette that he pulled from his breast pocket. He took a deep drag, leaned his head upwards and exhaled a long stream of smoke into the air. The breeze sucked it through the open balcony doors, dissipating the smoke almost as fast as he released it from his lungs.

"What else, Dunbar? I noticed no signs of forced entry when I walked in."

"Correct Commissioner Archibald, we haven't seen any signs of that either. This condo is seven stories up, so coming in through any of the windows, or even the balcony doors, seems unreasonable for a normal person."

"My thoughts exactly." Just then an officer interrupted their discussion, "Commissioner, the zealot has arrived."

Archibald dreaded the arrival of the zealot who was called to the scene, though he was the one who made the call. With a crime of this magnitude, his higher-ups would have torn into his ass had he not. He hated dealing with them, could smell the stink of their self-righteous attitude way before they silently arrived on the crime scene, under the mask of shadows. Archibald leaned to his right and looked over the officer's shoulder to see the dark silhouette of the aforementioned zealot standing in the threshold of the balcony doors, arms folded, his body language already screaming disinterest. They made eye contact, the zealot glided into the room with long strides. Acknowledging no one, he walked straight to where the conversation with Archibald and Dunbar was taking place. When he was within a few steps of them, Commissioner Archibald glanced at Dunbar and said lightly, "Could you excuse us for a moment."

Dunbar nodded and stepped away.

"What's good. Arch?"

"Santeaux. You're well aware that I hate when you call me that, let alone in front of my men."

"And you're well aware that I don't answer to you, so I don't care. You called me; I assume it's for a reason."

"You see the reason splattered all over this room."

"Obviously. The woman's face was split with a blade, one take."

"How do you even know that, you didn't even look at her?"

"You seem shocked Commish. I noticed that shit walking by, it'll take your CSI guys what, two to three days to come to the same conclusion I did within two minutes of being here? Dope team you got here, Archie..."

Archibald let out a gruff, inaudible sound and took another long pull of his cigarette, "Step into the bathroom."

"Whoa whoa, I'm used to getting dinner first, at least a dri..."

"Just go in the bathroom, asshole."

Archibald stepped to the side and let the zealot step into the bathroom.

"X, eh? Somebody's got some balls. Like, wooly mammoth sized balls to pull this shit off...Jesus Christ, he smells so bad."

"Santeaux, can you focus please."

"He smells like your mustache..."

"Santeaux, just fucking focus."

Myth quickly looked over his left shoulder at Archibald who was leaning in the threshold of the bathroom. His eyes and furrowed brow, the only visible portions of his face, were enough to convey how he felt about his focus being questioned by such an antique cop as Archibald. He returned his gaze to the body and began his assessment.

"I can tell by the state of his cuts that they were made one after the other, probably in 20-30 minute intervals. Left wrist, right wrist, throat, in that order. He was probably dead by the time his throat was cut, it looks like whoever did this was just frustrated at that point. The missing fingers…whoever did this was…"

Commissioner Archibald interrupted, "Trying to get Elizondo to talk, trying to torture information out of him."

"Well, Arch, you're not as stupid as you look."

1956

As the elevator lurched toward the unknown underground destination, Cyrus' heart was filled with uncertainty for the first time. All his life, he had wanted to follow in his father Francois' footsteps. Had he known that would include being driven into the middle of nowhere by two unnamed men and getting on an elevator to an underground bunker, he may have reconsidered his position. His racing train of thought was derailed by the commanding, yet endearing voice of the Colonel.

"Mr. Santeaux, Mr. Everett, life in the Arms Recollection Unit is not what you imagine it to be. By being here, right now, you are essentially giving your life to our mission. Trust me when I say: Many have died for this cause; the cause that President Roosevelt, God rest his soul, passed away envisioning would lead America to greater heights. You will be trained by some of the finest men the world has to offer. They will make you face the unthinkable, your own countrymen. Some people cower in the face of this concept. But any man, ANY man, that puts the betterment of our country in jeopardy is indeed our enemy. Rest assured, this is a war for the future of our country. The members of the ARU are zealots in the face of this hell. And we will emerge victorious..."

Just then the elevator slowed to a stop. The Colonel looked over his should at the two men.

"Allow me to introduce the men that will be training you."

The vertical seam where the doors connected began to part and light flooded the interior of the elevator compartment. The Colonel stepped off of the elevator first and walked down a small metal ramp.

There stood six men in a line. All were passing eyes over the new recruits, scanning them both from head to toe. One had a smirk upon his face as if to indicate to them that they should hop back on the elevator to avoid the embarrassment of imminent failure. Cyrus recognized one of the men as none other than Eliot Ness. Assuming that some stereotypes are based in fact, he imagined the Asian man to be the one in charge of the martial arts training. Cyrus' eyes darted around the room, trying to take in everything. The underground structure was massive, about the size of three airplane hangars. The entire area was divided into two halves, the training areas were on one side, and presumably the barracks and other structures were located on the other. Cyrus could see other recruits meandering about the double doors of the entrance to the living quarters, seeking the prime position to see the fresh meat that was about to be tossed into the grinder. There were large concrete walls separating the different training areas. The industrial style architecture made the underground bunker look more like a factory than a training facility. The ceilings were high, with huge hanging lights that illuminated the surroundings. He could make out what looked to be a dojo to his left. The hairs on his arm stood on end as he envisioned himself administering many a beating to his new fraternity in the ARU, and the uncertainty that he had felt on the elevator had immediately evaporated from his spirit.

The Colonel walked down the ramp and nodded in the direction of his six heads of command. They all saluted in unison, an indication that they were as disciplined as they were loyal.

The Colonel turned back towards the two new recruits, looking Gerald in the eyes, then shifted his gaze towards Cyrus.

"Gentlemen, the men standing behind me are tasked with creating a force that is unparalleled in its reconnaissance, firearms, and martial arts capabilities. Frankly, their job is to eat you alive, digest you, and shit you out. And out of that steaming pile of excrement will raise the finest operatives that this great nation has ever produced. You two men should know that the recruiters were sent out to find you based on our own research of your backgrounds. You are also here to replace the recently vacated positions."

Gerald looked perplexed, and couldn't keep silent any longer. The effects of his intoxication were left topside, his sober mind more prone to inquiry. He cleared his throat and spoke, "Colonel, what do you mean by recently vacated positions?" The six lieutenants chuckled to themselves. "Mr. Everett, the way we operate here is that, if we lose a recruit, we have to replace him. It is imperative that we steadily build our numbers and we can't afford to lose one man before the real battles begin."

The Colonel turned to walk away, but was interrupted by the unsteady voice of a now completely sober Gerald.

"Colonel...sir...if you don't mind me asking...what happened to the recruits that we're replacing?"

The Colonel swiveled his head around without turning his body,"Oh, they died. Follow me gentlemen."

The two new recruits didn't look at each other. They merely followed swiftly behind the Colonel.

The party proceeded at a brisk pace towards the dojo. Cyrus caught a glimpse of an ever growing crowd of loiterers gathering outside of the living quarters. They passed through a huge set of wooden double doors and entered the dojo. It was a large structure, much bigger than the exterior portrayed. There were four huge wooden beams that offered support to the high roof. The main area was nothing more than a huge square bamboo mat. There were some additional doors that Cyrus saw and immediately wondered where they led. An armory of hand held weapons ranging from kendo sticks and bo staffs to katana blades and nunchukus were on the back wall, each weapon resting perfectly on pegs that protruded from the wall. From their distance, it almost appeared the weapons were floating in mid-air. The Colonel walked to the middle of the room accompanied by his Asian Lieutenant, they turned and faced the two new recruits.

"Gentlemen, this is Xi Wang Xi. He is one of the most gifted martial artists the world has ever seen. He's been across the world refining his hand to hand combat skills. With his guidance, you will become human weapons. Trust me boys, this type of training is only to be found as part of the ARU."

When he finished speaking, the Colonel made eye contact with Xi and nodded in his direction. Xi was a clean cut Asian man that stood about five feet five inches. He appeared to be thin, but this was just camouflaging an incredibly powerful physique. He wore attire fitting of martial artists; black pants to match his black shoes, a robe-like top that covered his upper body drawn closed with a black belt. Xi stepped up to the forefront. He spoke in perfect English with a tinge of a London accent, taking both new recruits by surprise.

So much for stereotypes...

"You two blokes...to the center of the ring please." The two men walked toward the center of the room, where they could see red painted lines that indicated the boundaries of the sparring area. They turned to face their commanders and were greeted by, not only the Colonel, Xi, and the other five lieutenants, but also roughly 25 recruits that had jammed the entrance of the door, spilling into the dojo behind the heads of command. "My name is Xi Wang Xi, henceforth you will refer to me as Master Xi. The Colonel already alluded to this fact that I have traveled across this earth learning various styles and techniques that have made my body an instrument of death. My job is to give you something that other branches of the military do not. I intend to do that by beating the bloody hell out of you. Hopefully, during this time, you will gain something of value that will aid in you in the field. Please, face each other." Cyrus and Gerald were too entranced by the dojo, the asian man with a voice that didn't match his countenance, and the ever swelling audience to notice their bags had been taken from their sides, placed against the far wall as to clear the sparring ground.

"If you two would, on my mark, begin fighting." Cyrus looked perplex, "Sir...Master Xi, what are the conditions of victory?"

This inquiry garnished a chuckle from the lieutenants and the crowd of onlookers alike.

"Well chap, the next time one of you open your eyes; you'll be in the infirmary...making you the obvious loser." A seriousness befell Cyrus. He was confident in his hand to hand combat abilities, having received more training in his early childhood than most of the men that were present. Flashes of sneaking into the dojo after his father returned from the war filled his mind. His gaze turned towards Gerald, who was fumbling, trying to reach an object in the lapel pocket of his dirty green jacket. Cyrus watched Gerald's right hand disappear underneath his jacket, emerging with a small flask.

"Therrre she goes." Gerald muttered to himself before unscrewing the top and drinking the entire contents, his adam's apple bobbing up and down with each gulp of the presumably alcoholic beverage. Cyrus couldn't help but laugh internally. "What a fucking drunken nut case," Cyrus thought to himself, "he might as well sign his discharge papers now." Cyrus was becoming intoxicated with his own self-confidence as Gerald was achieving the same goal through different means. Cyrus' heart was now racing as he shifted his body into fighting position. Xi was also observing Gerald's peculiar pre-fight ritual, but his perception wielded a drastically different assessment of the situation. Xi was aware that the only men that were so brazen as to indulge in spirits before a fight were doing so because it would help them as opposed to hinder them. Xi Wang Xi knew Drunken Fist.

"Begin."

The words rang out like a starting pistol at an Olympic race. Cyrus looked up into the glossed over eyes of his opponent.

He's mine.

He dashed towards Gerald with three large steps, on the last step he leapt into the air with a double jump kick aimed at Gerald's mid-section. He was shocked when he didn't feel the impact on Gerald's body, who had quickly stepped out of range. Cyrus rushed again with a flurry of strikes that were hard for the gallery of recruits to follow with their eyes. Gerald wobbled side to side, ducking or swaying out of the way of every single strike. Cyrus could not discern if his sporadic movements were accidental or purposeful. Cyrus feigned a round house kick to throw his opponent off the anticipation of his attacks. He used the circular momentum of his body spinning around as extra force to channel into the strike he intended to deliver to Gerald. As Cyrus came out of the spin, he struck with a speed that made Xi, who was watching each recruit's moves intently, smile in a nod to Cyrus' execution. Cyrus felt the adrenaline fueling him, the sweat starting to leak from his skin. Everything else was blurred as if a veil had been placed over it, the sounds of the room now sounding muffled, though the recruits were worked into a frenzy by the display that they beheld. Cyrus felt everything moving in slow motion, his blow glanced past Gerald, who stumbled and spun with perfect timing. Cyrus could feel the hairs on his hand and forearm brushing past Gerald's face. Cyrus hopped backwards now, breathing heavily. He watched Gerald rhythmically stagger from left to right, hands in front of his face like a boxer with his fists only lightly clenched. Gerald slurred speech interrupted Cyrus' train of thought, "Shhall me

125

continue danshing?"

Before he could process another thought, Gerald was upon him. Cyrus was taken aback by his speed, taking consecutive steps backwards as Gerald unleashed a series of unpredictable strikes. Gerald's movements were confusing. As he swung a right handed blow towards Cyrus' throat, he stopped mid-swing and punched his ribs with a quick strike with his left hand. Cyrus blocked the next string of Gerald's offensive. He regained his footing and shot a kick toward the side of Gerald's skull like a rocket fired from a bazooka. He thought for certain it would connect but he was fooled again by the intoxicated ballet that his opponent was performing. Gerald twisted his body 180 degrees ducking beneath the kick. As Cyrus was carried around by the force of his kick he spun back to the forward position to be hit with a blow to the abdomen by Gerald, who was walking backwards with his back parallel to the ground, shooting rapid fire strikes into Cyrus's mid-section. Gerald's upper body weight, and undoubtedly all of the whiskey that he had consumed, forced him to fall on his back and roll to his feet, ending with his back turned to Cyrus. This angered Cyrus. He didn't come all this way to be made a fool by a lush such as Mr. Everett. He felt a sudden rush of adrenaline that was spiked with a rage that blinded him to the fact that one of his ribs was broken. He rushed in once more, when he was within one step, Gerald threw an elbow that missed its target forcing him to spin back to a face to face battle. Cyrus eluded the elbow by ducking underneath it, in that instant, he saw his opening. Cyrus stood and delivered an open palm strike to the sternum of Gerald. The pain from the strike sent Gerald stumbling backwards, a sobering remedy for his drunken state. Gerald gathered himself, but it was too late. Cyrus had rushed him with the same surprising speed that he was on the opposite end of just mere moments ago. Cyrus kicked his shin, forcing Gerald down to the floor of the dojo on one knee. An axe kick to the back of Gerald's head would ensure his trip to the infirmary. Cyrus didn't have time to celebrate his victory, nor did he feel like he was the victor at all. He coughed blood that sprayed onto the dojo floor. Shortly thereafter his vision faded to black. He collapsed, next to the man that he had just bested. The raucous cheers of the crowd that now surrounded the entirety of the square sparring area weren't enough to wake either man.

Xi looked at both men laid out in the square. He made eye contact with some recruits on the side and waved his hands towards them. The group hustled to the two men, carrying both of them out by their limbs towards the infirmary. Xi leaned over towards the Colonel and said lightly, "You did well with these chaps, sir."

"Quite well...quite well, indeed."

1997

Myth rose up and walked out of the bathroom with Archibald. They stopped just outside of the doors threshold, "So, the question is: what was the killer trying to find out?" Archibald asked aloud. Myth paused, then replied, "Had to be some valuable shit in order to go through these lengths to pry the info out of him. I mean, whoever it was strung X's stocky ass up like a piñata. What makes you do some shit like that? Like, where in the devious criminal manual..." He was interrupted by a visibly agitated Archibald, "Myth, please. The biggest mob boss in the Metro Corridor, maybe in the country, is rotting behind us. Cops hadn't even *seen* Elizondo in at least two years; whoever did this had inside information or was scoping X out for some time."

"Aww, it's always cute when you go into detective mode Archie. All that is true...but for me it's not the 'who' it's the 'what'. Whatever they were looking for, we're not even sure they found it. The only time an 'interrogation' of this type ends in death is when the information was obtained or it was clear that they weren't gonna get it. There has to be something in here, some indication of what X knew."

Both sat silent for a moment. Archibald took a notepad out of his coat pocket and jotted something down. Myth's eyes darted around the room. The crime scene investigators were still milling about as the blood of the murdered woman was beginning to congeal. Myth's eyes moved from her disfigured face, to the balcony door that he had entered, to the woman's hand. Her arm was hanging over the side of the bed, with her fingers hovering a few inches over the carpeted floor. Blood had dripped down her arm and pooled on the floor underneath her hand. Myth's eyes noticed the end of a piece of paper, rolled up into the shape of a tube, ever so slightly sticking out from under the bed, the very edge a dark crimson from the blood pool that it had touched.

Myth stepped towards a young man who was dusting a lamp on the nightstand for fingerprints, "Hey, umm, whatever the fuck your name is, could you stop doing the most stereotypical thing that you could possibly do when investigating a crime scene and pull up this comforter please?" The young man turned to see who had made this request in such a disrespectful manner. When he saw that the instruction came from a zealot, he quickly straightened up and obliged with a, "Yes sir." Myth knelt down to the ground and picked up the rolled up paper carefully as it had started to stick to the carpet, the woman's blood acting like an adhesive. He stood up just in time to be met with Archibald, who walked up. Myth unrolled the paper like a scroll. They both looked at it inquisitively. Archibald was the first to speak, "This is a blueprint of the subway. Why would Elizondo have this? Outside of the people that still live in base pop, the subways are barely used anymore."

Myth didn't respond, he continued to look over the map again and again. Five minutes passed, then ten. He analyzed the corridors, the sketches of the subway system resembling an x-ray of the city's body. There was a part of him that couldn't roll the map up and relinquish it back to the hands of the officers around him that were scurrying for clues. He took the small flashlight off of his belt and clicked it on. Then he pushed a button that made the standard light change to UV mode. His eyes widened at what he saw as he passed the black light across the surface of the map. Scrawled in the upper left had section of the subway map were these words:

And, behold, I, even I, do bring a flood of waters upon the earth, to destroy all flesh, wherein is the breath of life, from under heaven; and every thing that is on the Earth shall die. (Genesis 6-17)

By this time Commissioner Archibald had walked up to Myth, his eyes too saw the excerpt written on the subway map.

"It was written in an ink that is only visible under UV light. It has to be a lead as to what Elizondo knew. It's a passage from the Bible."

"Thanks Arch, I've never been a religious dude. I assume X wasn't either, considering the whole having sex with whores while married thing. That's not one of the commandments is it?"

Archibald let out an irritated sigh, "Not quite."

"I'm taking this map with me Arch. I'm gonna ask around and see if anybody knows anything. See? I can do detective shit, too."

This got a rare chuckle out of Archibald, "Take the map Santeaux, our guys will be in here collecting for another couple hours or so. We'll keep you informed on our findings. I assume that you will do the same."

"You assumed correctly," Myth said walking outside to the balcony. He was followed by Archibald.

"Myth, I'm serious. This is a big fucking deal. We need to find out what the hell is goin on here quick."

Myth didn't respond. Archibald retrieved another cigarette from his coat pocket. He cupped his hands to shield his lighter's flame from being snuffed out by the gentle night breeze.

"You know, you're dad was a helluva man, met 'em a couple times before he went off the grid. One of the best the ARU ever produced. Underneath it all, I know you're more like him than you'd admit."

Archibald raised his head and realized that he was the only one left on the balcony. Myth was gone as fast as he had arrived, as if he was never there to begin with. Archibald took another deep drag of his cigarette. He was joined by the head of the CSI unit, Dunbar.

"The team is doing one more once-over of the living room area. We'll be wrapped up in about 45 minutes. Sir, everything ok? "

"Yeah, Dunbar I'm good. Just trying to piece this thing together. Gettin' ready for this shit storm on the horizon."

Dunbar was slow to respond, "Yes sir. The murder of Elizondo will be front page news. I'm sure all the major bosses in base pop are chomping at the bit to take his vacant place."

"Yeah, that's true. But that's not all I'm referring to Dunbar."

"What else sir?"

"I'm fairly certain Elizondo was murdered by a zealot."

1957

The unmistakably gruff voice approached from behind with a loud whisper, "What ya' readin' there fucker?"

Cyrus turned his head, "I'm surprised you even know what a book looks like."

"Hey, hey now, you shouldn't judge a book by its cover. I do my fare share of readin' when I get the chance."

"I'm sure you're picking up Playboy for all the intellectual reading material."

"Of course. But mainly for the tits."

Cyrus and Gerald both laughed loud enough to disturb the other recruits who were in the study area, though, because the reputation of the two gentlemen making the friendly racket was already well known, no one would think twice of asking them to tone it down.

Cyrus had been in ARU training for almost a year now. He and Gerald had developed a strong friendship that stemmed from their sparring session that took place what seemed like ages ago. During this time, they had witnessed some 39 recruits fail out of training. For five of the 39, failing out of training also meant losing their lives. There seemed to be a constant revolving door of new faces coming in. It was the Colonel's words at work. Every recruit that left, either willingly, forcefully, or in a body bag, was replaced by another able bodied young man eager to prove himself. Cyrus smiled to himself every time he saw those elevator doors open, revealing the faces of men who, like himself upon his arrival, had no real understanding what they were getting into. He was used to the recruits gathering around for the sparring match of the new blood. He never took to that tradition. Instead, he opted to spend his time in the study reading up on various subjects. He would rather be in the dojo of course, but the raucous crowd that came to accompany each new sparring match, or Initiation Match as it was called, became annoying. The crowd seemed to be bigger and more boisterous each time in hopes that this new match would be the one that removed his battle with Gerald, a battle that had taken on folk tale type proportions within the facility, from atop its pedestal.

Cyrus marked the page in his book by folding the upper left corner down. He closed the book and asked, "How's the new blood looking? I saw the mob start to move in the direction of the dojo."

Gerald took a deep breath and exhaled, "Lookin pretty good. Muscle head types ya know? I dunno who told them that was all they needed to make it to the finish down here."

"Yeah, no shit. Remember that guy Greggs?"

Gerald laughed and lowered his head, "That guy looked like he could bench press life itself, and he didn't last 2 weeks down here. These guys should make for a good initiation match at least. I'm headed over there, might as well see what I'll be working with in basic H2HC class."

Gerald gave Cyrus a hard pat on the shoulder and rose up from the seat next to him, awkwardly walking towards the door. Cyrus thought to himself as he watched his friend walk out of the double glass doors of the study and into the mob of recruits how ironic it was that he moved more naturally when he was drunk out of his mind as opposed to when he was sober. Cyrus opened his book back up, smiling to himself at that thought, and continued his studies.

Cyrus was proving to himself and to his superiors that he did indeed belong in the ARU. He was excelling at each stage of his training. He was in the top five recruits as a marksman and arms specialists to go along with his already well-known fighting abilities. Xi had taken to Cyrus and Gerald since he witnessed them beat each other to near death during their bout. So much so that he enlisted the two of them to lead the basic hand to hand combat classes, after they were both fully healed of course. Xi had even went so far as to request that Gerald be given the opportunity to teach his Drunken Boxing technique, which was met with staunch opposition from other higher-ups, Elliot Ness especially, who had presumably already seen too much alcohol during his years chasing bootleggers during prohibition to welcome it willingly into the ARU. It would be the latter man's section of training that Cyrus was attempting to prepare himself on this day. Researching the exploits of "The Untouchables" during Prohibition, their techniques of seizure, the way they gathered information. He knew Ness would be especially hard on him. From the grumblings heard throughout the mess hall, Ness was none too welcoming of the new laws of the land, "All we had in those days were our wits and our sidearm. Now, I'm a smart man, and my brains did get me out of my fair share of problems. But that sidearm made me feel a helluva lot more comfortable doin' my job. I'm just not sure where this leads when we start yankin' guns out of people's hands." His trepidation aside, Ness was the instructor of the Reconnaissance and Apprehension section of the ARU training, and he took that job seriously. He knew what awaited these young men as they transitioned out of their training into real world missions, a real world that was steadily changing above them. It would be another year's time before Cyrus would experience what awaited him. All of his acquired skills would be put to the ultimate test. Those events would change his life.

1997

Myth moved across the city terrain, veiled in shadow, a blur in the peripheral vision of the many people that thought they saw something. He was moving so effortlessly, with such agility, it was amazing that his mind could be producing other thoughts aside from self-preservation as he navigated the heights of the Metropolitan Corridor. In fact, his mind was moving faster than his physical body. He was still trying to process the evidence that he picked up from the Elizondo crime scene. The subway map was burning into his brain. The zealot training had conditioned his mind to the point that he had a near photographic memory. The passage from the Bible was circling in his head. He could see the words in an endless loop, trying to find anything in their meaning that would help him piece together this puzzle. It was almost sunrise, Myth knew protocol was to return to the Mecca and report his findings to the tribunal. They certainly knew Myth and his team were deployed, and by this time they surely would know that Myth went to meet with Commissioner Archibald, so they would be expecting the intel soon, if not by sunrise. But something inside of Myth made him take a different route. He quickly ascended to the top of a small building, found a dark corner, and took a knee. He reached towards his ear to communicate with the other three members of his squadron. He pressed the button that opened the secure channel between his team, "Squad, this is your premier. Come in."

He knew his team was loyal, and that at any moment they would be responding. In quick succession, their voices each came through the communicator.

"Copy that, Raspy here sir."

"Solar reporting, Premier."

"10-4, Slant here."

135

Myth took a deep breath, as fast as his mind had been working he was drawing a blank at the moment. He knew the tribunal would eventually find out about an offense as egregious as withholding a major piece of evidence in a case of this magnitude. The tribunal would definitely reprimand him, remove him from the case, or worse. He quickly flashed back to his training days as a child at the Mount Z, the times he was made to kneel on uncooked rice for hours as punishment for insubordination. He quickly came back to the present moment. He felt a nervousness that he hadn't felt in a long time, coupled with an insatiable hunger to make the murder, the map, and the message scrawled on said map make sense. Deep down, there was another reason he wanted to pursue this lead so feverishly, a reason he wasn't ready to disclose to anyone, even his team. It seemed like forever, but only a minute elapsed before he spoke again, "You guys are to return to the mecca. I have some information gathering that I need to do. Any inquiries to my whereabouts, tell them to contact me via comm." Even as he said that, Myth knew that he was going to disable his communicator so that no one could contact him. For a split second he felt bad for misleading his team.

His team confirmed their new orders without question, another example of their loyalty. Myth rose to his feet, reached towards his ear and disabled his communicator. He felt the hilt of his katana with his finger tips then took a deep breath and exhaled into the night. He guessed that he had about three to four good hours until the sun came up. If he played it right, he could be at the mecca soon enough to not cause any suspicion. He knew he had to get moving, he was plotting out in his mind his route to Long Island, also known as Shaolin. There was an old acquaintance that he needed to speak with, and he knew that if anyone would be up at this hour, he would be.

1958--

    This was it. This was the moment that Cyrus had dreamed of since he was a child. He had flashes of seeing his father Francois' Purple Heart on the shelf at his home as a young boy. All at once he was that boy again, feeling those same emotions, wanting to make his father proud and prove himself to be a worthy successor to the ex-cop turned war hero. Cyrus was just assigned his first real mission since graduating, with honors of course, from the ARU academy. He had made it through the entire ordeal, earning the praise of his superiors along the way. Even Elliot Ness took a liking to him, sitting down with him on numerous occasions even after he passed his section of the training, going over the finer points of tactical reconnaissance with him into the late night hours. This was before Mr. Ness met an untimely demise in the field on May 16th, 1957. Something that made Cyrus wonder if the outcome would have been different had he been deployed with him. Maybe he could have saved him. Peers and superiors alike held him in high regard. He was eager to prove their praise accurate, deep down he saw his father's face on every one of them.

    It was late August of 1958 and the ARU was indeed in the midst of a war. The mounting casualties on both sides were proof of that fact. There was always a foreboding feeling that would accompany each raid or recollection mission. Sometimes, the offenders were easy to sway, surrendering their arms with little resistance and accepting the punishment for not willingly doing so when they had the opportunity. Sometimes however, the offending citizens were less than diplomatic. More and more people were joining militia groups, which were now considered terrorist organizations, to hold on to their guns. The National Rifle Association had become one of the largest such groups in existence, seeing their membership skyrocket after the arms prohibition legislation was passed. Members of the NRA did not see themselves as "terrorists", instead they considered themselves to be "freedom fighters", the last protectors of the liberties of the common man. Their decree that the United States government was on a slippery slope to taking *all* of its citizens freedoms was a lightning rod to those who may have been on the fence about abiding by these radical new laws, "The government is making it so that the common man can't even *protect* himself," was a common theme heard from supporters of the NRA. The NRA had gone largely underground, but they had cells in almost every state. Unlike the ARU, they didn't need to invest much time in actively recruiting, people came to them in droves. Militias that existed were quickly absorbed under the NRA umbrella. They had become the single biggest opposition to the ARU.

Cyrus got his mission briefing pamphlet and his orders two weeks prior to this day. He spent hours going over the intel that was provided. He was to join a group of some of the best ARU operatives that were available and head to a remote location in the Appalachian Mountain range where there was good reason to believe that a splinter militia had made the rural area its headquarters. He found himself now above ground for the first time in a very long time, enjoying the sun's rays and waiting with the other members of the 20 man squad that was getting ready to deploy. He was excited and nervous. He probably would have been more nervous had Gerald not been picked for this mission as well. As Cyrus was flipping through the mission pamphlet yet again and eagerly awaiting the humvee convoy, he caught the familiar awkward strut of his friend approaching him from the side.

"Damn, it feel like forever since I seen the sun," Gerald lamented.

"Tell me about it, you don't realize how much it stinks down there until you come up for some real fresh air."

"You look like an excited school girl out here. Did the quarterback just ask you to prom?"

Cyrus laughed, "Fuck you, Jerry. Besides, shouldn't you be getting prepped for this mission? Did you even read the mission brief that Professor Dell distributed to everyone?"

"Mission what? When did that happen?"

Cyrus sighed, "Well, at least I'm here to make sure your dumb ass don't die. I hope you got some--," Before he could finish Gerald had taken his trusty flask out of one of his pockets, waving it around, the sound of liquid sloshing back and forth proving it was near full.

"You might want to save that for the actual mission, knowing you though."

"You damn right. I've been sippin' on this for the last hour. Hey man, we're going into a warzone. I think God will understand if I wanna take the edge off a bit."

"I don't know if I'd call it a warzone, had you actually read the brief, what we're doing is kinda routine. Operatives all over the United States have been pinching these types of militias for a while now. I've heard that ARU squads twice as small have subdued militias twice as big as the one we're supposed to engage."

"Aw, look at you using you're big school boy words: subdued, engage," Gerald said attempting to provoke Cyrus into another friendly exchange of insults. Cyrus just smiled, shook his head, and continued flipping through the mission brief pamphlet as if he had not already memorized it. There was a long pause, Gerald looked down at the ground, took a sip from his flask and looked Cyrus square in the eyes. The fun loving nature that was usually present in his face was replaced by a seriousness that Cyrus found unsettling.

"Cy, you really think things are gonna be okay out there."

"Yeah, Jerry. Everything will be fine."

www.ingramcontent.com/pod-product-compliance
Lightning Source LLC
Chambersburg PA
CBHW071227260626
47162CB00004B/1454